Advance praise for: *the Accidental Audience*

"I enjoyed every second of it! Well-written, and a fun read."

—BRIAN McCULLOUGH, AUTHOR, *On the Edge of Now*

"Faith Wood created a detective novel gem in *the Accidental Audience* with lead character, Colbie Colleen, the female equivalent of Raymond Chandler's Philip Marlow. A finger-biting tale, it has all the twists and turns of a great detective novel. A must read!"

—DAVID TAYLOR

"A fun, good read. Favorite chair and coffee good . . ."

—FLOYD JONES, AUTHOR, *Blueberry*

"If you're looking for an entertaining story, this is it!"

—DENNIS CRAIG, EDITOR, *Pro Manuscript Review*

Gifted with Love
to Chelsea
Christmas 2017
May your life be full of love and
adventure
And your shelves be
filled with great books.
FaithWord

the Accidental Audience

the Accidental Audience

FAITH WOOD

Double Your Faith Productions
Airdrie, Alberta, Canada

the Accidental Audience
First Edition, Paperback, 2015

ISBN: 978-1511831345

ISBN: 1511831340

Printed in the United States of America

DEDICATION

With love, to my family and friends who encouraged me to follow my heart, and write a book I want to read!

May the people in your life treat you kindly, and fairly. May the choices you make be the right choices for you. May the surprises in your life be wonderful. Last, may you always travel roads that lead to wonderful adventures!

1

The jagged scar stretched from the underside of her wrist to just below her armpit. Surgeons said the dog ripped too much tissue, and they did the best they could—but no way could they sew her up in one straight line. Fifty-seven staples later and stitches too many to count, Colbie's arm resembled a craggy mountain range. She traced the thick, smooth scar with her fingertip, recalling her dad's words, "You'll have days made by the devil himself, Colbie Colleen, but you must be strong. Pull up your socks, stand tall, and get on with it," his Irish brogue ringing as strong as if it were yesterday.

He was right.

Recovery. Physical therapy. The pink slip. Of course, her C.O. said how sorry he was to cut her loose, but since she couldn't manage a firearm to safety standards, she had a choice of life at a desk, or taking a new path. The thought of being shackled to a slab of metal was repugnant, so the latter seemed the better choice. Either way, it was ten years down the drain. Her plan was to retire in her early fifties as a decorated officer with enough time left to enjoy life—the thrill of going to work each day rarely subsided, and six months ago Colbie considered herself lucky to enjoy her chosen profession. She delighted in debunking the myth that cops were only good for drinking coffee and eating donuts and, yes, there was stress, but not so much that she couldn't handle and compartmentalize it—an attribute she found handy on those few dark days.

"Heading out?" Sergeant Rifkin jolted Colbie from unpleasant recollection, snapping her back to reality. He knew his question was lame, but he couldn't think of anything else to say. It was a damned shame—he was losing a good officer.

"Yeah—I guess it's a good thing I don't believe in keeping anything other than the essentials in my desk. One box ought to do it . . ."

"Good . . . that's good."

"Do you want my plant?"

"Thanks, but I kill everything I touch. Even cactus."

"Me, too. I'm surprised it's still alive . . ."

"Right. Okay—well, I'll catch you later. Don't be a stranger." Colbie stood and shook his hand, thanking him for the last ten years.

And, with that, her career on the force came to an unceremonious close.

Decade done.

2

The physical therapist patted Colbie on the arm as a final dismissal. Six months later, she was done with physical therapy, free to move on with her life.

"That's it—you're done!"

"Really? I'm done?" Colbie pumped her fist as if she were lifting a five-pound weight. "You're sure?"

"You are, indeed—you'll have to keep up the exercises, but you can do those at home. And, if you're not already, I suggest joining a fitness center or gym. You'll be surprised how much exercising your entire body will help rehab your arm."

Colbie made a mental note to check out registration fees, but she wasn't sure if she could afford an actual fitness center. Now that she had to shell out money to pay for school, pinching pennies was going to be a way of life—at least until she completed her degree. She wasn't worried about shaking the few extra pounds from her usually slender frame—running would take care of that, and she could probably find some weights at a garage sale. So, when she thought about it, she couldn't think of a reason to pay for what she could accomplish outside and on her own.

"I'll check them out, I promise!" A quick hug sprinkled with last-minutes instructions, and Colbie was out the door to a new life.

****

By June, the scar receded significantly, and it was time to decide on a different career. She put it off as long as she could for leaving the force proved more difficult than anticipated; no matter how she tried to figure out her next steps, Colbie couldn't motivate herself to dive into something new. It wasn't until she rifled through her mom's hope chest looking for the pocket knife her dad gave her when she turned twelve that she discovered her life's direction.

A small box nestled among two sweaters and a wool blanket appeared untouched—clearly, it was placed there for safekeeping as its corners were pristine, original packing tape securing the top. Usually, her mom labeled the crap out of everything she wanted to keep as mementos—items of a practical nature were different than those with sentimental value, each tagged with pertinent information—when and where it was purchased, as well as how long it was used. Her mom's need to organize and label everything bordered on obsession—but, the hope chest wasn't large so only items of importance made it into the cedar-lined box. The small package, however, didn't have her mom's illegible scrawl, providing nothing to indicate its contents.

The pocket knife was exactly where Colbie thought it would be, crammed in the lower left corner of the chest. She hadn't thought about the knife for at least twenty years, and it was a bit of a mystery as to why she wanted it now. Yet, she couldn't get it out of her mind, and the two-hour drive to her mom's seemed an insignificant inconvenience in order to retrieve the gift from her father. She tested its blade on a stray piece of paper, then carefully sliced the clear tape on the small box, careful not to damage the package's contents. Her mom told her she could go through everything, and the cardboard yielded to a gentle tug as she carefully opened the flaps—there lay the drawings Colbie sketched as a child, free of creases, each separated by thin, parchment-like paper. Seventeen in all, perfectly preserved.

Her drawings of scarred trees and their subsequent individual rejuvenation transported her back to her youth, once again filling her with feelings of inferiority. Ever since she was a little girl, Colbie noticed things others didn't see or, perhaps, acknowledge. On family camping trips, she spent hours perched on a log or curled up in a lawn chair, sketching anything that piqued her interest—lightning-scarred trees—examining them with a detailed eye, noting the depth and extent of damage. New growth encircled the scars, allowing the trees to adapt to their new conditions, no two alike. Witnessing such regeneration was intriguing when she was young, and she gave little thought as to why she was so enamored with recognizing trauma and healing—back then it was just cool, and it was a fun thing to pass the time during the summer. As an adult, she marveled at the fact that nature created beauty amid such distress, always flexing to accommodate its new reality.

Perspective according to age.

The truth was Colbie's classmates considered her a little—odd—as she progressed through school, and she never felt as if she fit in. Her brother was the one who got the goods—quick witted, charming, and good looking—including their mother's favor. Her mother treated him as the golden child, showering him with devotion while offering little in the way of discipline. Girls in Colbie's class feigned friendship with her as a path to his highness, hoping for a glimmer of attention and a possible date. But it didn't take Colbie long to figure out their intentions and she soon retreated into herself, considering it a lucky thing that she didn't have any friends at all.

By nature, she was rebellious and, in her world, she endured constant criticism. She laughed too loud. Sang off key. Talked too much. No matter what she did, there was always something to irritate those around her and she felt as if she could never achieve a perfect balance. She was good at sports, but not an all-star—the harder she tried, the more she blended in rather than stood apart. As she matured, she practiced fading into the background, observing rather than participating, becoming nearly invisible in the crowded high school hallways. No one noticed her, and she found she could adopt an apparition-like existence on command, enjoying the anonymity it provided.

Other times, she was lost in the shadow world of her own creation.

It was sometime during her sophomore year when she realized she could recognize the shadow world in others—without considering age, Colbie quickly discerned the behavior and decision making of those around her. Psychics claiming to foresee the future fascinated her, as well as illusionists who created thoughts and environments they wanted others to see. Her world bloomed and she felt, for the first time, that she belonged; it wasn't until she studied hypnosis, mentalism, and forensic profiling toward the end of her police career that she began appreciating and respecting her ability to 'feel' what was important to others.

The need to navigate conflicts led to her polishing the craft she developed during youth while understanding her unique perspectives of the human spirit—and, through her curiosity, she created her own body of knowledge. The tree drawings solidified what she already knew but refused to acknowledge—her life was now, and always had been—about reading others. Profiling behavior. Anticipating actions. It was deep in her soul, and no matter how she tried to reject it, it always appeared as a comfort in her life. Class instructors at the Department veiled the art of reading people as something mystical and complicated, but Colbie understood they, as well as her colleagues, didn't appreciate that people were the sole reason they had their jobs. Without people's behavior, abhorrent or otherwise, every police officer would have little to do.

Regardless of the claims by her instructors, Colbie realized in the real world there are two compelling needs driving people: a desire to belong, and a desire for significance. She understood souls crave communities and with that understanding came the belief that once we have a place to belong, we need to believe we can influence something. We need to make our own decisions, be in charge of something, or be important to a cause—each reflects our need for significance.

And, so, it was a forgotten box filled with drawings of trees that inspired Colbie Colleen to immerse herself in her new life's path.

Psychological profiling.

****

"I don't know—it sounds screwy to me." Brian didn't believe in anything mystical and, to him, Colbie's plan to become a profiler represented nothing more than playing psychic.

"It's not screwy, and I think I'll be good at it. Look at the FBI—they sure as hell don't think profiling is screwy!"

"Yes, but this isn't the FBI. You can't work on the force, so what are you planning to do for a living? How are you going to make money as a psychological profiler?"

"I can't believe you're saying this—and, you're copping an attitude! Can't you just support me for once?"

"For God's sake, Colbie—think about what you're doing! How long will it take for schooling? After you're done with that, how long will it take for you to make a living—one that provides the money to pay bills? The whole thing doesn't make sense! And, let's face it—you're no spring chicken."

Colbie stared at her coffee cup, absorbing Brian's puncturing comment. She was stunned at his lack of support and sensitivity, and she questioned if there were an underlying motive. For being together eleven years, he certainly couldn't be surprised by her choice.

"What the hell, Brian! It's my life, and I'm sorry if you don't like it. I'm not asking you to be involved in it—I'm asking for your support. And, I shouldn't have to ask!"

She stood, her body poised for conflict. If Brian couldn't get behind her, how could their relationship survive? Her stance stood as a challenge, tempting him to take the bait.

Without comment, he gently pushed back his chair and headed for the back door.

"I'm out of here . . ."

****

Professor Burton droned on about the human condition, and Colbie couldn't have disagreed more with his assessments of anthropological behavior. He believed in the need for humans to lead a thought movement and instigate change, while Colbie believed humans seek to build a community before anything else. She also believed in what she calls the 'shampoo strategy'—lather—rinse—repeat. The way she saw it, if people followed her ideas, they would find it easier to navigate convoluted human behaviors described by Pavlov and Maslow, parroted back by milk-toast professors.

She watched and learned from her prof as he attempted to make his subject interesting. He and Colbie sparred often, and his attitude toward her made it clear he deemed her too uneducated—too pedestrian—to present a dissenting alternative. As she listened, her first boss's voice played in her mind.

What they think of you, her boss once lectured, *isn't your business—live your life in a way so no one believes the crap they say. Losing is not an option.* Then her superior officer tucked a small, torn piece of paper under the corner of her desk pad, tiny handwriting scrawled at an angle across its face:

When you come to the edge of all you know and you are about to step off into the darkness of the unknown, trusting in the universe is knowing one of two things will happen: one, there will be something solid to stand on. Or, two, you will be taught how to fly.

At first she wasn't sure what to make of it, but over time she understood the quote and why people make decisions and behavior choices. They act and react according to two specific 'drivers'—a desire to belong, and a desire for significance. Now, ten years later, the yellowing, tattered paper—some of its writing obscured by age—lay in a hidden drawer in her jewelry box. Every so often she read it, wondering if she could trust its sentiment—she wanted to embrace the wisdom, but terror prevented her from testing the philosophy given to her so many years ago. *What if it proves untrue? What if both things are untrue? Where does that leave me?* It wasn't the stepping off point that frightened her—rather, the aftermath of a crash landing.

She likened the quote to the crux of emptiness an addicted person faces each day—one day more toxic than the previous—and it was an albatross in her own life. Her addictions weren't for drugs and alcohol—they were for work, food, and exercise. All were means for escape and distraction, as well as opportunities to fill the emptiness. Colbie's in-service training taught her addicts use heroin, booze, and other substances to numb themselves, as well as to insulate them from a harsh, judgmental, and potentially unsafe world. Others choose a lesser route, such as tobacco or sex, but they are equally as dangerous. When she thought about it, she realized addictions are the same for everyone and, perhaps, we're not all as different as we wish others to believe.

Colbie snapped to as the professor dismissed class, her mind still considering belonging and significance were too important to ignore. She knew her instincts were right—when she coupled her beliefs with the quote from her boss, she discovered she could predict decisions and behavior choices of others simply by thinking about which of the two drivers were influencing them—somehow, it made everything easier to dissect. No, she didn't see eye to eye with her professor at all, and it was only in a pure moment of clarity that she realized how her own personal experience contributed to her easily interpreting human behavior.

Psychological profiling was no longer an interest.

It was her passion.

3

And so it went for another six months—school, work, and more school. Colbie was lucky to snag a part time job that was just enough to pay bills, but it left little for anything else—a situation Brian loathed and barely tolerated. He displayed his displeasure by spending as little time with her as possible and, as winter rounded toward spring, the weekend of St. Patrick's Day was no different.

"I'm heading out for a hiking trip with Ryan, and there are a couple of guys going whom I don't know—we won't get back until late Sunday night, so don't wait up. I'll have my phone if you need me."

Brian didn't look up as he delivered the news.

"That's cool—say hi to the guys for me!" She, too, didn't bother to look at him as he hoisted his backpack over his shoulder. She had no intention of calling him, and she was clear he didn't want her to.

“Schooner has an appointment this afternoon at the vet’s—the growth on his stomach is getting bigger, and we need to have it checked.”

“Fine.”

In true Brian style, he didn’t ask if she had the time to take the dog to the vet—he assumed if he weren’t around, she would do it. And that was part of their problem—too many assumptions, not enough consideration. Ever since Colbie announced her plans to pursue a career in psychological profiling, his behavior was cool, unconcerned, and distant, caring little about her plans for the future. He hated her dabbling in the occult—that’s what he called it—and she hated his complete lack of understanding.

“No problem—I’ll take him. I’ll call if something is terribly wrong . . .”

“Cool. Later . . .”

The door squeaked as it closed.

****

Colbie’s love for chess started when she was five—not because she was endowed with superior intelligence, but because there was nothing else to do but play cards and chess with her brother—chess was her favorite. It passed the time and, as she and her brother left puberty behind, Colbie understood navigating the delicate balance of human interaction and conflict was nearly the same thing as a chess game, strategy always at the forefront. Strategy with friends. Strategy with family. Strategy with life. Such understanding and belief lent credibility to her as a police officer for she was consistently required to think several moves ahead of her opponent. She deduced some people behave like pawns on the chessboard, recognizing only one strategy, one move, and progressing one step at a time. Others resemble the knight, appearing to move like a pawn then suddenly shifting left or right in the presence of opportunity. Then there were the castles and bishops—both opportunistic by nature—give them space and they will claim it immediately. Queens and kings have more going for them—people resembling these prized chess pieces approach life with flexible thinking, thereby evolving into a space of knowing what aids them in evasion, avoidance, or influence. All critical elements in the lives of many.

Learning how to distinguish the players in life was her reward—her gift—for hiding in the shadows and, during her youth, Colbie believed it separated her from a pool of possible friends. However, as a patrol officer, her insight offered a serious advantage. Yes, it made others nervous when she was around them—they thought she could see through them, and such clarity about their individual lives was unsettling. Conversely, victims and survivors adored her for they felt understood rather than persecuted.

Unfortunately, her colleagues lived life in a tunnel.

Colbie tried, but her coworkers never adopted her focus on life. Explore! Stop judging! Ask questions—don't pass sentences! Fact was her comrades—her fellow officers—were threatened by her fast-track ascent into leadership, and they flat out resented the little red-headed girl who made headway toward the goals they craved.

Alvin, in particular.

Alvin MacGregor—a strapping man who despised

Colbie. A woman with more seniority than he? It was impossible to imagine, and he constantly retreated into his own hate to deal with her success. From Colbie's perspective, he was unacceptably uncoachable, and consistently worked outside of his responsibilities and directives. His shadow side was insecure, convincing himself Colbie would actively stall any advancement to which he was entitled. To him, she was the constant chip on his shoulder.

No matter the circumstance, Alvin was argumentative with local youth, berating them so he could feel good about himself. He never attempted to build a sense of community, always believing he was superior to anyone else. Ratting out colleagues by informing senior staff they weren't carrying their weight held little remorse, and he could have cared less about the outcomes of such situations. To him, it was their problem.

Alvin's viciousness was unrelenting, but he displayed it in such a way that lent credence to his stories. Colbie's lying. Her gross incompetence. Her inability to function as a valued officer. For such venomous comments, Alvin spewed them with charm—he was charismatic and smooth, and he had an annoying way of convincing others of his feigned honesty.

A politician smile, and a politician style.

When his shift was over he often stayed at the precinct, citing his true passion for the job as a reason not to leave unfinished files. His odd behavior finally reached the point of bringing a sleeping bag to work, sleeping on the floor of his office. When cited for that behavior, he took patrol car keys home, or secured them in his locker to prevent anyone from leaving him in the office on the following shift.

Alvin's shadow world was one of manipulation,

malevolence, and malice, making his shadow self tough to manage—at first, Colbie reacted by fighting it. She argued. Rebelled. Pranked him with the help of other officers. But instead of forcing him to shift his behaviors as she hoped, it only made him worse. Finally, she realized his craving for significance, and she started stroking his ego whenever she could. She ignored the unacceptable behavior, and commented on his positive performance. She handed him the responsibility for vehicle maintenance, forcing other staff to check in with him so he would feel like he had a level of influence and control. Her strategy worked for the best since no one else wanted the thankless job anyway, and it proved worthwhile. Eventually, she appealed to Alvin's competitive nature by broadcasting she was interested in a special ops assignment she didn't want. Then, she talked to the supervisor in charge of that group, begging him to take Alvin off her hands. It worked. Alvin transferred, and Colbie's superior officer once again validated her intuition and insight regarding navigating Alvin's difficult behavior.

When Alvin caught wind of it?

He was pissed.

****

"Ryan? Hey, it's Colbie. Is Brian there?" Colbie switched the phone to her left ear, ready to scratch down notes, if needed.

"Brian? No—we got back this afternoon, and I dropped him off at his car. Why?"

"This afternoon? He's not home yet, and I'm getting a

little worried. I'm sure it's nothing—he probably had things to do before coming home. Thanks! Sorry to bother you!"

"You're not . . ."

Colbie clicked off before he could say anything else. This afternoon? *Where the hell is he?* Her thoughts tangled as she rewound their last conversation. Granted, they didn't part for the weekend on the best terms, but he was seldom late coming home, especially on a Sunday night. Especially when he had to be at work for the mid shift at eleven o'clock on Monday. She played his usual Sunday routine in her head, trying to figure out what could be taking him so long, and it took her little time to figure out something wasn't right. Although she couldn't pinpoint her fear, she felt as if she were peering into the devil's closet.

No—something wasn't right, at all.

4

Sunday inched into Monday without word. It wasn't Colbie's nature to do nothing, and her onslaught of calls to Brian's family and friends yielded little—no one heard from Brian since Friday with the exception of the guys who went on the hike. Since she didn't know a couple of them, she relied on Ryan's getting the word out that she was worried—but, because they returned several hours earlier than expected, she didn't have a handle on how long Brian was really missing. She wasn't expecting him until after ten—but, if he got back to town at four o'clock? It provided ample time to vanish without notice . . .

Colbie held scant hope that Ryan would actually text or call her, or his friends—she spoke to him three times throughout the night and, by the third call, he gave the distinct impression he understood why she and Brian were having problems.

Now, she was on her own.

Brian's Monday shift didn't begin until late morning,

so it seemed prudent to wait to contact his boss—she didn't want to look like an idiot girlfriend if Brian simply decided he needed time away from her. As an ex-officer, she knew the drill—he had to be missing for forty-eight hours before they could issue a BOLO and Missing Person's Report. After all, she could be making something out of nothing.

Colbie's training and experience should have helped in this situation, but she found herself gravitating to what she felt rather than what she knew. As an officer, she was trained to look at the facts, but her intuition was telling her something different. Still, she advised herself not to panic, and she refused to call Brian's phone every five minutes—but, by noon, she caved and called Brian's boss.

"No—I haven't seen him yet. He's usually not late, but maybe he had car trouble or something."

"Did he indicate he was planning on being back to work today?"

"Nope. I didn't even know he was going anywhere."

"Well . . . thanks. When he does arrive, will you please ask him to call me? If it's not an imposition, I mean . . ."

"Sure. No problem." Colbie carefully recited her number, requesting him to read it back. No use taking any chances of his transcribing it incorrectly, but she knew in her gut she wouldn't hear from him again.

As of one o'clock, Colbie knew two things—Brian returned to his car about 4:00 P.M. the day before, and he was missing. The realization of the actual number of hours since his return to town tossed her stomach as she considered the possibilities, none of them good.

She tried to piece together snippets of past

conversations with Brian, but there were challenges linked to being a cop and an intuitive—each yanked against the other as she assembled her mental puzzle pieces, hoping to stumble upon some sort of clue. Instinctively, she knew Brian was in trouble, yet there was no way to sync her feelings with her police training.

By dinnertime, panic. Nothing from Brian. His parents were out of the country, so contacting them seemed of little use, and his sister wasn't concerned when Colbie called. Clearly, it was up to Colbie to make the first move.

She dialed the precinct.

"Sarge? Colbie. I need a favor . . ."

****

Sergeant Rifkin sensed urgency in her voice, knowing Colbie wasn't one to be alarmed without provocation. She explained the situation as if she were still on the force, reciting the facts in her non-nonsense, cop-style manner.

"I know—forty-eight hours. But, damn it, Sarge, there's something wrong. I feel it . . ."

"When did you last see him?"

"Saturday morning, about nine-thirty. He left to go on a hike with a few friends—he mentioned he didn't know a couple of them, but they were going with one of Ryan's friends. Ryan is Brian's closest bud—they've known each other for ten years."

"Did you speak to Ryan?"

"Yes. He said they got back earlier than expected, and he dropped Brian off at his car around four o'clock on Sunday. He hasn't heard from him since." Sarge listened as Colbie relayed the contents of conversations with Brian's friends and family.

"Okay—what haven't you told me?" No matter his confidence in his former officer, he knew she was functioning in a heightened state of emotion, and she may forget important information.

"Nothing. Except that Brian and I haven't been getting along the best since I left the force. He's had a difficult time adjusting . . ."

"Adjusting—what does that mean?"

"Just that he isn't on board with my career choice."

"Are you sure he isn't seeing someone else?"

"Brian? Good God, no! I think all of this is just a bump in the road. Besides, with my ability, I think I'd know if someone else were in the picture."

"Well, that makes sense. Where are some places Brian hangs out?" With that, Colbie launched into a complete narrative regarding Brian's habits—watering holes. Restaurants. Friends. Thirty minutes later she clicked off, relieved there would be progress, and she would no longer carry the burden herself. There was a slight comfort knowing the guys on the force would place her at the top of the list.

She was right. Word circulated quickly about Brian's vanishing and, as anticipated, her colleagues rallied and initiated an extensive search.

By Thursday, still nothing.

It was time to order cell phone records, and apprise Brian's parents and sister—if she could find them—of what was happening. Ryan was in on the search from the beginning—it didn't take him long to jump on board after he learned his friend hadn't been seen or heard from since he dropped him off on Sunday. He no longer viewed Colbie's distress as that of a distraught girlfriend—not hearing from Brian for twenty-four hours was one thing. After that? Ryan didn't know what happened, but he surely needed to find out.

****

"Okay—let's write down what we know. What we don't know, too . . ." Ryan decided to take a couple of days off from work in order to search for Brian, and meeting with Colbie was his jumping in point.

"I did, but I didn't come up with anything."

"Then let's go over it again. We know I dropped Brian off at his car around four o'clock on Sunday. I unloaded his backpack, and threw it in the backseat while he checked to make sure he had everything. We talked for a minute, then I took off. I didn't see anyone, or anything that made me suspicious or uneasy."

"Was anyone else in the parking lot?"

"Not that I noticed."

"How many cars?"

"Maybe ten. Twelve. Not many."

"Describe the cars you remember . . ."

"I didn't pay attention . . . but, there was one parked in the far corner with no other cars around it. While the car sticks in my mind, it might mean something—or, nothing."

"What did it look like?"

"Green. A Subaru, I think. Ski rack on top."

"Year?"

"Not sure, but it was older. An older Outback . . ."

"Was Brian the only one with you?"

"Yeah—I didn't have to drop off anyone else."

Colbie scratched notes on a legal pad as Ryan relayed everything he remembered about that day.

"What about the two guys you didn't know? What's their story?"

"Kirk and Vinnie? I don't know much—they're friends of Alex. They seemed okay to me—Kirk is kind of quiet, and he didn't have much to say. The other guy, Vinnie, was the opposite—loud. Boisterous. A know it all. Both of them knew their stuff, though, and they were as skilled as the rest of us."

Colbie sat back, tapping the tip of the mechanical pencil on what was left of the legal pad. Everything Ryan said made sense, but she still sensed something was off. The hiking trip. New guys. She shuddered, an ill wind passing through her as she envisioned their trip.

"What do you know about either of them? Anything?"

"Not much—Kirk works in computers, I think, and Vinnie is an outdoor guide. Where, and for whom I'm not sure."

"You mean he's well-versed in survival techniques?"

"That may be going a little far, but he definitely knew his way around a campsite. He was set up before the rest of us, and he took the first watch."

"Bears?"

Ryan nodded. "We didn't see any, but one of the Wildlife guys told us to be on the lookout—there were more sightings than usual within the last couple of weeks, and they're getting more aggressive. Cubs, probably, although it seems too early to come out of hibernation."

Colbie clicked the mechanical pencil for more lead.

"Did you like him? Vinnie, I mean."

"He was alright, I guess . . ."

"You guess?"

"Yeah—I can't put my finger on it, but there's something . . . different about him."

"What do you mean, 'different?'"

"He was kind of aloof. Stayed to himself, and really didn't try to engage in conversation—but, when he did talk, he was loud. Now that I think about it, being obnoxious is kind of weird for a guy who is an outdoor guide. He looked and acted like a man with a lot on his mind."

Colbie and Ryan sat in individual silence until finally calling it a night around ten-thirty, neither knowing much more than when they started in the early afternoon. Colbie's legal pad was filled with names, arrows, and question marks—most of her scratchings resembling hieroglyphics to the majority who might read them. Bits of shredded paper littered her kitchen floor, the aftermath of her heightened concern and worry. According to Ryan, the hiking trip was uneventful—each man was there for his own reason, one of whom was disinterested in campfire conversation.

That was about it.

Colbie locked the door as Ryan disappeared into the shadows of the quiet street. She watched as he hoisted himself into his truck, blowing on his hands to warm the bite of the raw evening air. She was disappointed when he couldn't recall anybody or anything in the parking lot where Brian left his car—so far, all she had to go on was an older model Subaru Outback. Nonetheless, it was worth a morning drive to check it out.

****

She maneuvered her car into the northwest corner of the parking lot for optimum surveillance. Two businesses shared the lot and, judging by the names on the front lawn sign, she figured most of its tenants and their employees worked a usual business day from eight to five. From her position, she had a view of the entire lot with the exception of five or six spaces on the far side of the building. By seven-thirty cars began pulling in, filling the lot by a few minutes to eight. Colbie watched each driver carefully, taking notes and jotting down observations—Ryan was right. Nothing seemed out of the ordinary.

By eight-thirty, two spaces remained—one next to her, and one on the far side of the lot. At eight thirty-five, a forest green Outback swerved into the space beside her, nearly clipping her front left fender. Before Colbie could say anything, the driver's door swung open and a svelte, thirty-something woman sprinted toward the building, perhaps late for work and oblivious to Colbie's watching her from her car. Skinny jeans and heels accentuated the woman's height, as did the midi-length leather coat. Blonde hair streaked with cherry red shone in the sun, her sense of contemporary style on display for anyone glancing her way.

She dripped confidence.

Colbie watched as she disappeared through the front door, then shifted her attention to the car next to her. The Outback was an older model, matching the description Ryan gave during their marathon brainstorming session. She pegged the car to be a '97 or '98, its passenger side rear bumper creased by something narrow and slender, and a long scratch etched the driver's door. Clearly it was a car belonging to someone who cared little about its appearance—strange, especially since the young woman dressed with class.

She scribbled down the license number knowing the guys on the force would run it immediately. As she pulled away, her Spidey sense alerted her to the necessity of further investigating the tall, sleek woman.

5

Colbie stopped by the precinct on her way home. No sense waiting—if there were something interesting about the young woman in the green Outback, she wanted to know immediately. Her gut told her the woman knew something about Brian, but her brain held back. After all, she didn't have anything concrete, and if it were anyone other than Sergeant Rifkin, her intuitive abilities wouldn't count for much.

She sat on the bench outside of his office, thinking about the tall woman.

"I didn't think we'd see you around here again—how's retirement?" Alvin's voice behind her grated on her nerves just as much as it did when she had to work with him.

"I didn't retire."

"Well, I figure it amounts to the same thing."

"My life . . ."

Rifkin's door opened, signaling her to enter. Sarge never escorted anyone through the door, inviting them to sit down. If the door opened, that was the cue to get her ass in there, and don't waste his time.

"Gotta go!" Grabbing her purse, she headed for the door.

Alvin's annoyance was clear—he needed more time to grill Colbie about Brian. News of Brian's disappearance grapevined through the precinct and, even though he could care less about her boyfriend, it was wise to be up on important cases. Based only on the fact that Colbie was in Rifkin's good favor, it was a given that anything to do with her or Brian was going to be top priority. At least for a while.

"I hope you find him . . ."

"How do you know about that?" Colbie pivoted, squarely facing her long-time adversary.

"Everybody knows—any luck?" Colbie couldn't quite grasp his sincerity, and she wasn't sure it suited him well.

"No—nothing yet."

"I'm sorry . . . well, let me know if there's anything I can do."

You're sorry? Colbie muttered her thanks, stunned at Alvin's concern. But before he had a chance to say more, his cell vibrated—he gestured goodbye and dismissed Colbie with an arrogant wave, answering only after she was out of earshot.

"Hey, Baby . . ."

****

Rifkin impatiently motioned Colbie in and closed the door behind her, watching closely as she chose a familiar chair.

"What?" He knew that look.

"What do you mean, 'what?'"

"You always chew your lip when you feel something, and you were chewing your lip just now. What's buggin' you?"

"I don't know—something is off." Her conversation with Alvin quickly rewound in her brain.

"I'm sure it's nothing—I chew my lip?"

"Yes. Now, why are you here?"

Colbie launched into a recap of her surveillance of the parking lot, the green Outback, and the stylish woman.

"Plate number?"

"Colorado 758 XDN."

"Colorado? Interesting—I wonder what she's doing here?"

"I don't know, but she's interesting enough that running the number might be just what we need to learn something about Brian."

Rifkin agreed, rapped on the glass, and held up a piece of paper containing the license number. The officer on the other side acknowledged, copied the number, and turned to his computer—within moments, he was knocking on Rifkin's door.

"It's registered to a Nicole Remington. Age thirty-five. Blonde." The officer handed Rifkin the information, waiting for further instructions. At Rifkin's direction the officer retreated, closing the door quietly behind him.

"Well? What do you think?" Colbie couldn't wait for Rifkin's response. "May I?" The sergeant handed her the printout.

"That's her. She has bright pink—kind of a cherry color—in her hair now, but that's the only difference. I figured she's in her thirties. She's tall, but holy crap—5' 11"? She was over six feet in those heels!"

"You know we don't have any reason to investigate her, right? All you know is she was late to work, and that's not exactly the best reason to launch an investigation. You don't even know if she were late—could be she was right on time. And, you don't know if she knows Brian . . ."

"I know. I know! But, I feel it. Somehow, there's a connection, and I think we need to dig deeper into . . ." Colbie glanced at the printout. ". . . Nicole Remington."

"Okay. For now, we'll keep an eye on her. But, if within a week we don't have anything, we'll need to move on. You know that."

"I know. That's okay. I'll do an investigation of my own, and I'll keep you apprised of what I learn about our mystery woman."

"Mystery woman?"

"Yep. I'm thinking there's much to learn about Nicole Remington—I know there is."

Agreeing to keep in touch, Colbie left Rifkin's office

with renewed motivation and resolve to find out about the woman driving the green Outback, and how she connected to Brian. *Maybe she doesn't have anything to do with it,* she thought as she pulled onto the street.

Then again, maybe she does.

****

There was no avoiding it—Colbie had to contact Brian's parents and sister about his disappearance. She never did get in touch with his mom and dad the week before, and the conversation with his sister didn't go well. Even so, she owed it to Brian to do as much as possible, and she knew he would want her to reach out to his family.

She dialed.

"Good morning. May I speak to Mr. Cauldwell, please?"

The voice on the other end spoke in broken English making it difficult for Colbie to understand, and after a few minutes of getting nowhere she gave up, no wiser about how to get in touch with Brian's parents. She left her cell number with the housekeeper, knowing she wouldn't hear from her. Now, with hope gone for Brian's parents informing his sister, she took a deep breath, and pressed enter to connect. His sister's phone rang five times before patching into voicemail. Colbie left a message, stressing her concern about Brian, and asked for a return call as soon as possible.

Now, she was on her own. Knowing the workings of a police precinct, she understood help from her fellow officers would decrease soon, and eventually Brian would fall off the grid. As of now, she had to do as much as possible, as soon as possible, and she'd start by staking out Nicole Remington.

****

She eased left onto a city street lined with Victorian brownstones and bare-branched trees. Still early spring, trees were only thinking about budding—but Colbie imagined the street when trees were in full bloom. *Impressive*, she thought. *And, expensive*!

Several years passed since she was in that part of town as an officer investigating a domestic dispute, and it changed little since then—the only differences in the row houses were varying shades of brick caused by years of weathering. Yet, it was a pricey area, making her wonder what Nicole Remington did for a living, and how she could afford such extravagant digs.

Inching the car down the narrow street, she scanned each brownstone for the address she memorized when in Rifkin's office. Officers at the precinct wanted to help as much as possible, but the fact was they had old and new cases to investigate, and it would only be a matter of a couple of weeks before they put Brian on the back burner. It was up to her to generate leads in an effort to keep the officers engaged and in her corner.

Colbie skillfully maneuvered into a small parallel parking spot only slightly up from her targeted address—a perspective from which she could see the comings and goings of nearly everyone on the block. A shadowy feeling nudged her to believe the row of brownstones would be the first break in the case—how and why she didn't know. But, she felt it.

She settled in for a long wait, rifling through her purse for a sandwich bag filled with peanuts. As an officer, whenever a stakeout was necessary she expected to miss meals, so peanuts and a couple of slices of cheese kept her going. Same deal for her current surveillance. It was already four o'clock, and she suspected Ms. Remington would show up sometime after five—if she were lucky. Having a bite to eat now meant she could wait several hours in her car if she had to—still without guarantees her suspect would come home.

Questions knotting in her mind, she jotted them down as they came to her—*how can she afford such an expensive place? Who pays for it? Does she pay for it on her own? If someone pays rent for her, then who? Who owns the building?* Clearly, her suspect must earn a hefty salary in order to afford such a high caliber residence. The understated elegance of the brownstone fit her Ms. Remington's personality—what she knew of it so far, anyway. The cut of her clothes. The expertly applied color in her hair. The way she walked. Each belied a born elegance and breeding—if she did have something to do with Brian's disappearance, it wasn't a slipshod operation. It probably took money—and, connections.

That thought concerned her.

It was a risk, and Colbie hoped she had enough time to check out the names by the building's intercom callboxes before Remington got home. The street wasn't brightly lit, nor was the entrance to Remington's flat—better for sleuthing. In less than a minute, she stood in front of the list of names seeking confirmation of Remington's living there. *Let's see—Brownburg, Jamison, Carson, Marshall,*

Vincent, Remington. Pay dirt! Colbie memorized the list of names, and hurried back to her car to settle in for what could be a long evening.

Before long, residents trickled in and lights flickered on, sheer curtains drawn to protect privacy. It wasn't until five o'clock that Ms. Remington zipped into a parking space four down from her front door.

Different car.

This one was a late model BMW the color of melted milk chocolate, meant for taking corners at high speed, thereby eluding anyone who may be in pursuit. Colbie knew little about cars, but she knew enough to know the car cost bucks. Lots of bucks. Ms. Remington's wasn't the type of car afforded by a moderate budget, so she obviously made a mint in her job, came from money, or both.

Colbie scrunched down in her seat just enough to maintain a view of her target and the brownstones as the suspect took her time getting out of the car, chatting on her cell and completely unaware of any surveillance. Colbie previously lowered the driver's side window a tad to avoid fogging, and she clearly heard Remington's voice as she passed in front of Colbie's car.

"Friday? I think that works . . ."

Excellent! Plans for Friday! Catching that snippet of conversation provided another link to the case—*who was she meeting? Are they involved in a personal relationship? Business?* Colbie watched as Remington energetically mounted the steps of the brownstone. *Odd,* Colbie thought. *I don't have that much energy when I finish a day's work—did she work today?*

A fine drizzle froze on her windshield as the temp

plunged below freezing. Such cold temperatures in early spring weren't unusual, but Mother Nature's timing could use a little work—the defrost worked only sometimes, and within a couple of minutes damp condensation formed on all windows. By five-thirty, it was time to pack it in. It wasn't a sure bet Remington was going to stick around in her brownstone for the rest of the evening and, with the weather turning, she figured there wasn't much more she could do that evening—until Remington emerged from the brownstone looking like a model from the best red-carpet runways.

Colbie's suspect crammed a letter into the outgoing mailbox, flitted down the steps, eventually folding herself into the BMW. A call on her cell. Checking her makeup in the rear view mirror. Seatbelt. Colbie scrunched further in her seat as Remington eased the sports car from the tight parking space with precision. *She's driven that car before,* Colbie thought as the car moved toward the end of the street. Again, her thoughts raced as she considered how the lovely Ms. Remington could afford such luxuries. The car. The brownstone. The sleek, polished style. Perhaps all was not as it seemed—*a possible sugar daddy for the long-legged lady*? Colbie's increasing questions warranted further investigation, and she couldn't wait to discuss the little she knew with Rifkin. But, would her findings be enough to keep her fellow officers on the case? All she could do was hope . . .

She pulled out after the BMW, hoping Remington didn't recognize her car as the one beside her in the parking lot where Ryan dropped off Brian. She stayed just far enough behind as not to arouse suspicion, following for a little more than ten miles outside the city, and into a rural area. *Where the hell are we*? She thought she knew most of the areas outside the metro because of her time on the force, but these roads were unfamiliar—so many turns. Unless a person happened upon the spot by mistake, there was a scant chance of finding it.

Colbie slowed to a crawl as the BMW pulled into a long lane flanked by bare trees and winter crocuses poking through remnants of snow. Within moments Remington curved out of sight, forcing Colbie's hand to follow or not. Pursuit at this point was a recipe for disaster—a risk Colbie couldn't take.

In the waning light, desperation surrounded her. A cold prairie punctuated with clumps of trees lay before her, lending to the feeling of hopelessness snaking through her body. Except, it wasn't her hopelessness.

It was Brian's.

Colbie eyelids fluttered, and in her mind's eye she viewed Brian tied to a straight-backed chair, his head drooping lifelessly against his chest. She felt his misery. His anguish. His despair. The vision intensified as he moved through her, his life force weak and on the precipice of death.

Time was running out.

****

His parents flew in from Spain as soon as they heard the news their boy was missing, his sister a no-show. She had the courtesy to send Colbie a text explaining her reasons for staying put—her parents could hold down the fort and, besides, what could she do except hold their hands? To her, the whole thing smacked of babysitting, and it really wasn't her style. All Colbie could do was text her with new information, but the truth was her texts would matter little, and she was beginning to think Brian and his sister weren't really related.

As her investigation entered its second week, interest in the case at the precinct was beginning to fade. Colbie caught wind of a rumor circulating through the various departments that Brian couldn't stand being with her anymore, and simply split the sheets. Oh, there were a couple of the guys who still had him on the radar, but by the tenth day of his disappearance, Colbie sensed she was on her own.

Ryan distanced himself, as well. Private conversations with his friend several weeks ago revealed a mounting dissatisfaction in Brian's personal life, but he didn't go so far as to mention making alternative living arrangements. Even so, Ryan entertained the idea it was possible for his friend to make himself scarce until he decided on a course of action. Still . . . it wasn't like Brian to take such a cowardly way out. It was more like him to face the conflict head on, and deal with the fallout like a man. No, there was an element of truth in Colbie's words, so he requested she keep him regularly apprised of her progress. But, that didn't mean he had to spend much time with her.

So, there she was—solo. Colbie's first surveillance op on Nicole Remington didn't yield much—all she really knew was Remington had expensive taste in cars and fashion. And, she visited someone out in the boonies. Colbie didn't dare follow her down the lane for fear of being discovered, but she did make a visit to the City Planner and Zoning Office to pull the plat for the address and surrounding area. She also knew Remington had plans for Friday, offering another opportunity to gather additional pieces to the puzzle. Deep in her gut she knew Remington was in it up to her eyeballs, and she wasn't going to quit until Brian was safe.

6

Friday dawned as unsettled as days previous—drizzle, fog, and spitting snow made for good reasons to stay inside, but that was impossible. Colbie still wasn't sure of Nicole Remington's employment, and her vision warned of passing time as well as an undesirable result. It was imperative she confirm Remington's working in the parking lot building—if she didn't work there, Colbie had much more on her plate. More surveilling. Longer hours. Less time.

No matter how long she stood at the bathroom mirror that morning, her reflection remained static. Prominent charcoal-colored circles creating a hollowed look to her already thin face belied her confidence that neither police nor she would locate Brian before it was too late. Brian's parents turned out to be totally worthless when it came to adding a beneficial contribution to the search. After spending time with them, Colbie speculated about where Brian got his intelligence—perhaps genes way down the line. But, in an effort to maintain her sanity, she promised to keep in touch with them throughout each day as assurance of progress. When it came down to it, Colbie and a few cops were the only investigators on the case.

Not nearly enough.

The blustery weather lasted throughout the day, developing into a full-fledged early spring snow storm by midafternoon. Colbie figured it was more important to tail Remington at the end of the day when she would be more likely to meet friends for happy hour—but, the weather may cause her to change plans. Remington's appointment to meet someone on Friday she knew about—with whom she didn't have a clue. Or, what time. Staking out the parking lot from two o'clock on seemed a wise approach, and a crapshoot at best. Since she still didn't know where Remington worked, arriving in the afternoon allowed time to wander through the building to see if she could locate her mark—which office, Remington's employer, and any other tidbit of information she could gather.

By the time she pulled out of the driveway, the storm was in full swing, snow swirling in all directions as she navigated through snarled traffic. The office building was only five or six miles from her place, but it would take at least forty-five minutes to get there—if she were lucky. A few cars in front of her fishtailed as they hit the binders, unaware of black ice underneath the thin layer of snow. Conditions couldn't be worse.

The parking lot was emptier than usual, perhaps due to the weather, but the green Outback was parked in the same spot. *Why does she drive the Subaru to work, and the BMW for play?* Just because the car was there, however, didn't mean Remington was anywhere in the vicinity—she could have left it there, or abandoned it. One thing was certain—it was time for answers.

It was also time for a little acting.

As Colbie ascended the outside steps, an unmistakable tremor coursed through her as a warning something wasn't right. She paused, allowing her vision to take shape—Remington and a man who seemed familiar to Colbie. His features were undefined, but she had a distinct feeling there was a connection to a foreign country. Italy? Not sure.

She sat on a park bench outside the front door next to a cylindrical ashtray, its white sand stuffed with lipstick-stained cigarettes. Relaxing her body and mind, Colbie encouraged her abilities and, for a brief few seconds, it were as if she were watching a movie in her mind. Yet the images remained opaque and vague. Remington. The house. Brian. This time, he was staring straight forward as if concentrating on something directly in front of him. He appeared stronger, and not so resolute to his fate. His color was better, and it was clear someone was feeding him as well as taking care of his basic needs. *Why? Why is someone putting him through this? What could Brian possibly have done to warrant this type of torture?*

Then it was gone. Colbie opened her eyes, taking a few seconds to focus on the present—the bench, the ashtray, the massive steel-framed entrance doors. She sat, gathering herself, for the first time fully aware Remington was at the heart of Brian's disappearance. Her initial assessment was correct—Remington was in it up to her eyeballs.

Armed with new resolve, she pulled open the giant doors.

"May I help you?" The receptionist had a pleasing voice, slightly nasally with a timbre of youth.

"Well, maybe—I'm thinking of leasing office space in

this area, so I'm doing comparisons. Although, I probably didn't pick the right day for it!" Colbie laughed as she glanced outside. She learned a long time ago receptionists know everything going on in their buildings or individual offices. A good receptionist is privy to variegated gossip, and the position is fraught with providing advice to those who seek her wisdom. On the surface, receptionists appear non-threatening—the truth is they perform their duties with an undercurrent of inexplicable power.

"I know! I'm not looking forward to my drive home!" The receptionist flashed a toothy smile, engaging with Colbie as if she were an old friend.

"So, do you like working here?" Interrogation started.

"It's okay—I mean, it's like most receptionist jobs. The building staff is great, though, and they take pride in keeping it clean. The last place I worked, I'd be lucky if my trash were emptied every day!"

"You're right about that—it looks great! What kind of businesses are here?

"There are several, but the biggest one is the real estate company on the third floor. There are also a few doctors, a chiropractor, and several consulting firms. Business professionals mostly . . ."

"It sounds as if I'll fit right in—I'm a psychologist."

"Really? Cool—you will fit in!" Another broad smile.

"And, real estate? That's interesting—I've been thinking about making a move to this side of town, and I'll have to find a good realtor." Colbie grinned at the receptionist. "Ugh—moving! I don't even want to think about it!"

"Well, if you do decide to move, I know one of the agents upstairs is supposed to be pretty good—Nicole Remington."

"Remington? Never heard of her—why do you think she's a good realtor?"

"Oh, I hear things—not too long ago, she received some kind of top producers' award, so I guess she must know what she's doing."

"You'd think . . . well, I don't want to keep you from your work. Thanks for being such a good ambassador for leasing space in this building!" Colbie turned as the front door opened, sweeping in snow and a blast of frigid air as automatic hydraulics slowly closed the door behind a timid-looking delivery man clutching a bouquet of spring flowers. He hesitated as he checked the name of the recipient.

"Flowers for Nicole Remington. Should I leave them with you?" Colbie waited as the receptionist accepted them, then placed a quick call to the third floor.

"Hey, Jasmine—will you please tell Nicole she has flowers waiting for her at the front desk? Thanks . . ." She hung up, turning her attention to Colbie.

"You can speak with her now if you want—Jasmine said Nicole will be down in a few minutes."

"I appreciate your effort, but I think I need to make it home before the roads get too crummy. Thank you, though!" Colbie had no intention of letting Nicole Remington so much as get a glimpse of her. As long as she remained anonymous, she could continue her surveillance—as soon as Remington noticed her, all bets were off.

The elevator dinged as Colbie pushed on the heavy

front door—she dared not look back. Her back to the receptionist, as she adjusted her gloves she noticed the cigarettes in the outdoor ashtray. Without thinking, she snatched one and headed for her car she purposefully parked out of the line of sight of anyone at the front of the building—the more unnoticed she remained, the better.

Snow and ice froze on her windshield making scraping necessary—*I really needed to get the defroster fixed,* she thought as she chipped at the stubborn ice, unaware of eyes watching her every move.

Nicole Remington made a mental note—according to the receptionist, the woman scraping her car may be a new client.

Then again, maybe not.

7

"I'm just not comfortable with this—I don't care what you say, this is going south and you're not taking me down with you!"

"Who said it's going south? Everything is going as planned. C'mon Baby . . ."

"Come on, my ass! I have a lot at stake, and I have a hell of lot more to lose! How long has it been since you've been out there, huh? I'll tell you—days. Nearly a week!" Remington seethed as she took to task the voice on the other end.

"How do you know it's her?"

"Believe me, I just know—same car, same slight build, same auburn hair. You don't have to be a genius to figure it out!"

"Well . . ."

"Well, nothing! End it. End it now!"

8

Alvin closed the door quietly behind him. "Hey, Sarge—do you have sec? I know you're busy, but I was wondering if there's any progress on Brian's case. I haven't heard much going around the precinct . . ."

"It's not a good time, MacGregor—I have a press conference in fifteen minutes." Sarge hated press conferences, always regarding them as a necessary evil. More often than not, they interfered with his investigations and he'd much rather keep progress on his cases close to the vest.

"I'll be quick. Since you put the guys on new detail, is there anything I can do to help?"

"That sounds a bit odd, don't you think? Coming from you? It's not a little-known fact you hate Colbie's guts."

"I don't hate her . . . it's weird, though—since I don't have to work with her every day, she doesn't piss me off nearly as much."

Sarge tipped his chair onto its back legs, loosening his tie. He didn't believe in looking like a stiff in a suit for the press and, besides, a loose tie made him look as if he'd been working countless hours—which he had. Murder is never a pleasant thing, and he had every available officer on the case. Alvin was right—Brian's case was at the end of his priority list no matter how much he didn't like it.

"Nothing new."

"Leads?"

"Not that I know of—Colbie hasn't been in touch for days, although I know she's working on it on her own. I suspect I'll hear from her soon."

"Well, when you do, let me know if I can help. I'm a good cop and, as a good cop, I have to put my personal feelings aside. If you need me to work on Brian's case, let me know." Alvin stood, keeping his promise to respect Sarge's time.

"Maybe. Now, get out."

****

Colbie and Ryan wrapped their hands around mugs of hot chocolate as Colbie related her experience at the office building.

"I was stunned when I heard she was in real estate, let alone a top producer! But, when I think about it . . ." Colbie's voice trailed as she envisioned the possibilities. "I mean, how else would anyone know about a home that's off grid? Well, not really off grid—but you know what I mean."

"I admit, it makes sense. What I can't understand is why she's involved in the first place. What does she have to gain?"

"I don't know—I considered that. As soon as I got home, I researched her real estate career—she's a big deal, and her success explains the expensive car and snappy clothes."

"Why didn't you find her on the Internet before now? I don't know you well, but I can't imagine you wouldn't have Googled it the second you learned about her."

"I did—a Nicole Remington showed up, but she looked completely different. The Nicole Remington, real estate broker, had dark hair and weighed about fifty pounds heavier. There wasn't any resemblance, at all. I figured it was a coincidence . . ."

"Now that you know where she works, do you think she's the same woman?"

"I don't know—I'm just not sure. See? What do you think?" Colbie fired up her laptop, and brought up her search for Nicole Remington. "See what I mean? Does she look like this woman?" She slid her phone across the table, a picture of Remington walking up the brownstone steps cued on the screen.

He studied both carefully. "No, not really. I can see why you didn't put it together—neither would I. Maybe she's not the same woman . . ."

"Maybe. But, think about it—two women, same name, same career, within fifty miles of each other? It's one hell of a coincidence if you ask me."

"I agree—it is possible." Ryan wasn't sure what to

think—he knew Colbie's reputation as a good cop, and he knew now to trust her instincts. "What's next? What are you going to do?"

"Well, the first thing is to fill Sarge in on my progress. After that, I think I'm going to need your help—I can show you the location of the country house on the map. Since someone might—although doubtful since it's in the middle of nowhere—recognize my car, I need you to do some poking around. See if you can engage neighbors in conversation, if there are any—and try to find out who lives there now. I couldn't find a record of a recent sale, so it may be empty."

"I can do that—tomorrow? I'll clear my calendar at work, and take a sick day."

"Good. I really appreciate your help—from here on out, we have to work as a team. My gut tells me it's the same woman, but why would someone go to such lengths to change appearance? Running from something, perhaps?"

Convinced of Remington's involvement, within the hour she laid out her plan to Ryan. Her best friend offered her car earlier that week in case Colbie needed a vehicle no one would recognize—it was time to take her up on it.

Before Ryan left, they made plans to meet the following evening. Each had marching orders, and it was critical they touch base at the end of each day.

Now there were two on the case.

****

Precisely at seven-fifteen the following morning, Colbie opened the door of the precinct. Shift change was over, and chances were good she could catch Sarge before he started a day of press conferences and directing the murder investigation. The last thing she wanted to do was run into Alvin for she knew he would try to get his two cents in about Brian's disappearance.

No such luck. He stood at the water cooler on the way to Sarge's office, and there was no avoiding him. Colbie steeled herself against the impending verbal assault.

"Madison! You look tired." The snotty look was the same, and Colbie cringed at his calling her by her last name.

"Alvin. I am tired—thanks for noticing."

"No offense. Any word on Brian? I guess not, or you wouldn't be here."

"It's nice you know exactly what I'm thinking." Colbie refused to let him bait her. "I'm working on a few leads, but nothing concrete yet." It galled her to explain, but at this point, she could use all the help she could get—even his.

"I know we haven't been close—in fact, we despise each other. But, when it comes down to it, you're a cop, and you'll always be a cop. It's my duty to help a fellow officer—so, what do you know?"

Colbie's first instinct was to blurt out her findings about Remington, but she wisely reconsidered. Yes, it would be nice to have help, but Alvin was never sincere before, and it was unlike him to be sincere now. No—best to wait until she was sure she could trust him.

"I'll let you know—thanks."

“Fine. I’m available if you need me.”

They parted on somewhat amiable terms, Colbie still trying to figure out what he had up his sleeve, if anything. Maybe it were possible for Alvin to help her—in many ways, he was a good cop, and there was an off chance he could be an asset to the investigation. But, she’d have to think about it. There was the adage about *keeping your friends close, and your enemies closer* to consider—she had to admit such pearls of wisdom had merit.

Nearly a half hour later, Rifkin emerged from his office, motioning her in, same as always.

“What’s up? It’s been a while—what’s the news on Brian?” Rifkin looked as if he took a couple of turns in the wringer—gaunt, exhausted, and out of ideas. She knew the drill—he was on twenty-four hour duty, and it showed.

“Get a load of this . . .” Ten minutes later, Colbie took a breath. “Can you believe it? I’m heading to the realty office after leaving here—not the one where she works now—the one she left before coming here. I think I’ll get more information there, and I want to find out why the hell she underwent such drastic facial surgery. I mean, you should see her—she literally looks like a different person!”

“Keep on it—if I can let any of my guys go, I’ll have your back.”

“I appreciate it—remember when I always told you, I can feel it?’ Well, same thing here—I feel it.”

“I know . . .”

****

Colbie and Ryan met at Draco's, a quiet tap on the east side. Stress etched both of their faces, but neither exhibited the tells of throwing in the towel.

"Sarge told me if he can let loose of any of his guys, he'll put a couple on our investigation. With the murder and everything, I'm surprised he's willing to make such a commitment."

"Does he buy into the theory that Remington might not be the person everyone thinks she is?

"He didn't say one way or the other—but, if he's willing to throw some officers our way . . ." Colbie paused, considering the possibilities. "So, what happened on your end? You didn't happen to see Remington, did you?"

"No. But, I did have a chance to talk to one of the neighbors—a neighbor who lives little more than a quarter of a mile from the location of the house in question."

"Does she know Remington?"

"Kind of—she knows *of* her."

"What does that mean?"

"Well, she was a bit on the weird side—the shotgun at her side was my first clue. As soon as I pulled in the driveway she was out the door, standing in front of the car with a *don't come any further* look on her face."

"Holy crap!"

"That's not all—when I started to get out of the car, her dog appeared. Not just any dog—a mammoth German Shepherd with an obvious distaste for trespassers."

"What did you do?"

"I raised my hands—I felt as if I were in a grade B western—and, as soon as I did that, she backed off. Then I popped the question, 'Do you know Nicole Remington?'"

"And?"

"She commanded the dog to lie down, and asked me what I had to do with that bitch."

"What? Seriously?"

"I'm not kidding! Her exact words were, 'That bitch? Don't come another step!' I told her I didn't have anything to do with her—and I explained everything while standing behind the driver's door of the car."

Colbie sat back, stunned at Ryan's story. "What does she have against Remington?"

"Turns out the lovely Nicole Remington is the demon nemesis of land owners—she snatches up land foreclosures in the area and, for the last couple of years, she's been putting pressure on land owners to sell, taking full advantage of a tanking economy."

"Why? What's so great about the land out there?"

"I'm not sure and, when I asked, she clammed up."

"Altogether?"

"Yep. Until she told me to get off of her property."

"I gather you left . . ."

"Of course I left! You think I was going to stick around chatting with a woman who could—and would—command her dog to attack? Or, shoot me in the ass? I don't think so!"

"Well, I can certainly relate to the attacking dog thing

. . ." Colbie subconsciously placed the palm of her hand over the scar extending the length of her arm.

"Clearly, there's something about that property—something we need to find out. Problem is, I'm not quite sure who to contact. Or, about what . . ."

"My guess is there's an added value to the land no one knows about . . ."

"Such as?"

"Oil, maybe? Minerals? Treasure?"

"Oil? You think?" Silence. "If that's the case, then I need to contact a geologic surveyor. You don't happen to know one, do you?"

"No, but I might know someone who does . . ."

By the time homemade mud pie arrived, the conversation turned to Colbie's investigation of Remington's former employer, which turned up nothing. It was tour day for the agents, and the receptionist was the only one there—and, she wasn't talking.

"I don't know—there was something about her that raised my antennae. She didn't have a receptionist kind of look . . ."

"A receptionist kind of look? And, that is . . .?"

"I'm not sure I can explain it. This woman has an undercurrent of intelligence about her—and, distrust."

"Is that your intuitive side talking?"

"Probably—but, you know what? After all these years, I know to listen to it. There's just something about her . . .

anyway, I didn't stay long because I didn't want to tip my hand. I used the excuse of needing to find a place to rent, and the receptionist told me to come back the following day. So, that's what I'll do—I'll go back tomorrow."

Coffee. A nightcap. Plans. Colbie and Ryan parted at the close of the evening, determined to make progress the next day. Ryan was to check out the geologic surveyor lead, and Colbie would head back to the real estate office. As they confirmed a phone call for six o'clock the following evening, Colbie questioned whether Ryan truly knew the peril of his best friend.

How could he?

9

She kicked off the covers as the vision formed and percolated in her mind's eye. Everyone was there—herself, Ryan, and Remington. Brian. Each wearing a blindfold, sitting silent and stationery as if cemented in time, neither acknowledging the other, separated only by ignorance. A ticking clock, its hands spinning around the circumference gaining a frenzied momentum each time they passed twelve. Alvin.

Colbie lurched awake, her nightshirt clinging with sweat, hair plastered to the back of her neck. Tremors twitched her muscles as she attempted to orient her conscious mind, unsure of what she just witnessed—she should have known her senses would explode with information as lay down to sleep. By purposefully bypassing her conscious mind, she tapped into her place of peace and comfort—and, information. She'd been there many times when needing to heal her mind and body by her own intuitive wisdom and, as she descended into the depths of her soul, she felt as if she were in the presence of an old friend.

This time, however, was different. There was an urgency—an impression of emotional chaos—propelling the vision, casting a sense impending critical mass. *Why blindfolds? Why weren't they moving? Why Alvin?* Right now, none of it made sense. The only thing Colbie understood was what she suspected all along—time was running out.

She also understood her vision was a revelation.

****

Keeping a class schedule was nearly impossible as the search for Brian progressed. Colbie almost cashed it in by contacting the Registrar's Office to call it quits for the semester. She called, but the person on the other end convinced her there was a solution to her problem—online. The university offered online instruction for each of her classes, and by taking advantage of the online service she would free up valuable time for the investigation. It was worth a try—she had to do something, or her money for that semester would be down the toilet.

Most classes were audio lecture, except one—Behavioral Abnormal Psych, and her class was the first of three sections with Professor Blackwell who preferred video to audio lectures. His exams included trick questions to ensure students actually viewed his lectures, and they weren't based on the obvious such as what he was wearing that day. No, his questions required students to think and explore the possibilities of the mind, and how they affect human behavior. His reputation was legendary, his classes at the university always full.

Colbie clicked the play icon.

"Today's topic—*Willful Blindness*." Blackwell's voice was smooth, yet strong. "If I say the word *blindness*, different images materialize for different people based on their own past perceptions of what blindness means to them. Perhaps you think of Helen Keller, or maybe you think of a grandparent who is blind. Or, you envision a person walking down the street with a white, red-tipped cane. Each of us is different." A pause. "So, what does this have to do with you? Well, think about this . . .

Some of us are God-fearing people, and some of us are God-loving people. Some of us are atheists, and some of us are in between. Some of us hold onto the hope that Thomas the Apostle made it into heaven, and so will we. Yet, all of us have a blind spot—perhaps more than one—in our lives." Colbie scratched down notes as the professor lectured, circling the words *willful blindness*, punctuating them with a question mark.

"There are various levels of blindness, but today's topic—willful blindness—isn't a physical phenomenon, although it could manifest itself with physical attributes. No, willful blindness takes over when an individual has the power to allow light to penetrate thought in the form of knowledge or fresh data. Think about that—*the power to allow light to penetrate thought in the form of knowledge or fresh data.* But, here's the kicker—individuals *choose* to remain in darkness. Why? Because, sometimes, it's the easiest thing to do. Or, they linger in darkness to avoid making a decision—a decision that makes them uncomfortable. Willful blindness is when the light of *knowing* is there, glowing brilliantly—yet, when we reach for and grab the brass ring, we extinguish that light. *Willful blindness is the moment we grab that brass ring, and pop off that light.*" Professor Blackwell paused a moment to take a sip of water. It were almost as if he were standing in front of her, behind a lectern, and she were his only student—such a feeling of intimate learning was not only a surprise, but a clear benefit of online learning.

"Just as there are various levels of blindness," he continued, "there are various levels of darkness. If *total blindness* is the complete absence of form and light, with little or no perception, then what is *willful blindness*?" The professor made the most of a well-timed, dramatic pause. "Just this—willful blindness oozes into daily life like a cracked egg through one's fingers while preparing breakfast. You knew you should have cracked that egg gently into a bowl with two hands, but you chose to do it a la Julia Child with one hand. Ah! And, there you have it! Yellow yoke, and clear goo seeping through your fingers."

Colbie stared at the screen, no longer taking notes, her mind flooding with instantaneous clarity. Everything began to make sense—last night's vision. Remington. The blindfolds.

The professor continued. "You see, willful blindness is a choice—we choose to not see, reason, or listen to an inner voice. We choose to allow our personalities to control bad choices—to choose willful blindness—while placing values on a convenient shelf. We often choose willful blindness knowing the outcome will cause conflict. Recall the example I used about the egg yolk—the knowledge of the possibility of breaking the yolk was present. Yet, that knowledge did not supersede the possibility of the yolk breaking, thereby persuading the person breaking the egg to do so with two hands. Generally, people perceive conflict as a bad thing rather than to try to see it as an impetus for change.

There is so much we read about in today's world—we wake up to horrifying, beautiful, and mediocre news. We awake with the choice before us to move toward action inspired by what we hear. But, most of us just shake our heads, making *tch-tch* sounds, and do nothing. Some of us have jobs requiring us to make decisions that affect our employers, our co-workers, and, perhaps, even the world. When we recognize something is a little off, or rubs us the wrong way, do we take decisive action even if it means we might experience some type of discomfort? Probably not. What do we choose? *Willful blindness.* We choose willful blindness by willing ourselves to look the other way. We hope someone else will come forward. We wish the issue will resolve itself—quietly."

The lecture continued for another thirty minutes before the professor doled out questions to be completed in essay form, and submitted by the end of the following week.

"In closing, brilliant students, I will leave you with this—rearranging one's entire life to keep one's eyes wide open rather than eyes wide shut is not an easy endeavor. Willful blindness is as strong as a hurricane setting its sights on a specific target—sometimes it can't be avoided. The good news is everyday life choices fall somewhere in the middle, and those choices don't have to result in total destruction. Simply recognizing the choice opportunities in front of you is half the battle—you can choose willful blindness, or not. Sun Tzu in The *Art of War*, chapter three, paragraph eighteen states, "If you know the enemy and know yourself, you need not fear the result of a hundred battles."

Colbie stopped the video as the professor bade good day to his students, her brain reeling with a new revelation—the intensity of her vision the night before was directly related to Brian and his disappearance. Those in her vision were participants in willful blindness—all members of an accidental audience willfully unaware of what was happening around them.

She sat back in her chair and closed her eyes, envisioning herself taking off a blindfold. As light engulfed her, Colbie understood Nicole Remington's Achilles heel—her willful blindness. For the first time in two weeks, Colbie understood—not everything, but she knew Remington was the tip of the iceberg and it was time to discover her reasons and motivations for participating in Brian's disappearance. The *how* was no longer imperative—it was the *why* stepping into the light, taking center stage. Colbie realized Remington's willful blindness centered around making bad choices for the sake of money—no surprise there. The car. The clothes. Her style. But the real revelation was understanding Remington's willful blindness was also her weakness. If there were such a crack—a chasm—in her personality capable of bilking unsuspecting landowners of millions of dollars due to oil speculation, then she'd crack and sing like a canary about who was behind Brian's disappearance. Nicole Remington wasn't as formidable as Colbie once thought—in fact, Colbie sensed Remington's fracturing under the pressure, exposing weakness and fear.

It was time to grill everyone who saw or was with Brian during the week of his disappearance. So far, her investigation was all wrong and, even though she and Ryan gained pertinent information, it wasn't enough. Now, everyone was a suspect.

Time to start over.

10

Colbie reviewed her list of everyone who saw Brian within a forty-eight-hour period before his disappearance, checking off those who clearly didn't have any idea of what happened. Ryan's friend, Alex, as well as his two friends, Kirk and Vinnie, were with Brian immediately before his vanishing, and she needed to concentrate on them. Then there was anyone associated with Nicole Remington—it was imperative to dig deeper into Remington's real estate deals to ferret out anything lending credence to Ryan's suggestion of homeowners unwittingly sitting on a boatload of money. During the early stages of her investigation, she didn't consider such a convoluted mess. Now? Worse.

Winter turned the corner to spring that week. Soft spring grass resembled green velvet as it stretched across lawns and early gardens, the freezing drizzle and snow a fading memory. Brian's parents, however, didn't get to experience the new season—they bagged it as soon as the temperature hit twenty degrees. They instructed Colbie to keep them posted about each step of her investigation no matter how seemingly insignificant—with the caveat, of course, they may be difficult to get a hold of due to no cell service on the island. Colbie could, however, leave a message with the housekeeper. Colbie dutifully agreed knowing how well that went on the first go-round, and wished them well on their voyage. She thought better of offering to keep Brian's sister in the loop for doing so would be nothing but a meaningless exercise. Even so, Colbie felt oddly rejuvenated—with the changing season, there was also a freshness to her investigation. Her vision reaffirmed her belief that Brian was still alive, and she knew she must be painstakingly careful in her investigation from that point forward.

Evenings were the most difficult—too quiet. Too empty. Brian's energy was still strong and, even though they were going through a rough spell, she knew in her gut their relationship was worth saving—accepting its demise was unacceptable. She crawled into bed that night, mentally prioritizing her to-do list for the next day—first, call Alex to ask him to meet her at the coffee shop on First and Cross at three-thirty. She counted on it's not being too crowded because she needed to surreptitiously record the conversations, and the din of crowd noise wouldn't help that effort. Although he probably wouldn't mind being recorded, plopping a recorder on the table lent an air of police investigation—just what she didn't want to happen. Conversations with each suspect must be as comfortable as if they were sitting at the kitchen table, or like best friends talking at the end of an evening out. From experience, Colbie knew achieving such an element of comfort was easier said than done—slap someone in an interrogation room, and they usually did one of two things—spilled their guts, or clammed up.

No taking a chance on the latter.

Colbie switched off the light on her nightstand just as her phone vibrated its notification of an incoming call. She considered ignoring it, but when the vibrating ceased and started again immediately, she recognized the code—ring twice, hang up, ring again.

"Ryan? Hey—what's wrong? Did something happen?"

"Sort of . . . I saw Nicole Remington at the Rio del Sol."

"What? Tell me—everything!"

"There's not a lot to tell, except she was with some guy, and they seemed to be involved in a deep discussion."

"Who? Have you seen him before?"

"No—but, there was something familiar about him. I'm not sure why . . ."

"Familiar how? What does he look like?"

"A big guy—solid. Red hair—or, it used to be red. He had grey hair by his temples. Fair complexion."

"Do you think their evening out was personal, or business?"

"It seemed personal. Remington looked upset and, at one point, she left the table. But, maybe she just needed to use the ladies' room—I don't know."

"What time were they there? I'll check with the restaurant in the morning to see if they made a reservation under his name."

"I knew you'd ask me that—I checked my watch when I saw the maître d' seat them. Ten o'clock."

"That late? Seems an odd time for a business meeting, don't you think?"

"That's what I thought."

"What time did they leave?"

"I don't know—we left before they did."

"That it? Is there anything else?"

"Only one—I saved the best for last. The guy who was with her? She called him Al."

"Al? Are you sure?"

"Yep—I heard it as I passed their table. I took the long route to the restroom . . . she said, 'Damn it, Al!' as though she were really pissed about something."

"Really?" Colbie's wheels were turning. "Interesting. Anything else?"

"Nope—just thought you should know."

As Ryan clicked off, Colbie attempted to sort out and make sense of what he just told her. Curiosity overwhelmed every rational thought of simply hitting the sack for a good night's sleep, so she plumped her pillows, making herself comfortable—no reason to wait to invoke her perceptive mind. This time, however, she wouldn't concentrate on Brian—now, Nicole Remington was the target of her intuitive scrutiny.

Her muscles relaxed as she allowed her mind's eye to serve as a movie screen. At first, she didn't tune in on anything in particular—over years of self-training, she knew to enter her psychic space slowly. Without intent. She must trust the knowledge within her to present itself at the right moment, and at the pinnacle of her reception.

Colbie lay motionless on her bed, envisioning her feet wrapped in a brilliant white light, inviting it to travel the length of her body, cocooning it in its soft energy. When fully encased, she surrendered to her mind's eye, knowing just the right time to ask for answers to her questions—it were as if she felt nothing but warmth, love, and spiritual awareness. The more she relaxed, the more her mind and body prepared to accept the answers that were sure to come. At precisely the right moment, she requested only good and valid information to remove the possibility of a negative force coming through. Usually, answers to her questions presented themselves as symbols, and it was up to Colbie to interpret them correctly. Sometimes there was only one, sometimes several—she never knew what to expect.

Aware her intuitive mind was open, she fired her first question—*how is Nicole Remington involved in Brian's disappearance?* Within moments, images of crosses appeared on the screen in her mind, dotting an expansive area. Not religious crosses for she experienced no feelings of a spiritual connection. No, these were crosses that resembled the letter 't', and there were many—twenty. Maybe thirty. She made a mental note of what she saw in her mind's eye, knowing objective interpretation wouldn't come until later. Colbie knew better than to put her subjective thoughts and beliefs into her reading process—the chance of misinterpretation was too great. Mix truth with what she thinks is truth and the reading would be inaccurate, the process squirreled.

The scene of the crosses lingered then dissipated into nothingness as another took its place. A hammer ride at the amusement park. Scotch plaid. Colbie couldn't quite discern whether she were viewing a blanket, or maybe a dress. Or, skirt. The image vanished as quickly as it appeared leaving her with a dark viewing screen, indicating the information regarding Remington's involvement was complete.

Next question—*who is helping Nicole Remington?* Immediately, her viewing screen exploded from black to a vivid crimson as her body braced against a strong, consuming force. Shards of crimson hurled from a tornadic vortex shredded her screen, coming together only to disappear and respawn. The vision repeated several times before vanishing into itself, self-destructing, forcing Colbie to abandon the reading. *Holy crap! I've never experienced anything like that—ever!* She lay still, making certain her breathing was evenly paced in an effort to calm her racing heart. *What the hell was that?* The ferocity of the vision was stunning, and she wasn't quite sure what to make of it. Its sheer strength was unsettling—did her guarding against such negativity fail? Her prayer didn't work? One thing was certain—Colbie knew there was a driving force behind Nicole Remington, and it was unrelenting. Fierce.

Evil.

****

The coffee shop was a ghost town except for a few stragglers who looked as if they camped there for hours engrossed in their laptops, tablets, and phones. The only chatter was between two baristas, and Colbie could barely hear them as she strategically chose the table in the furthest corner from the cash register. The small partition wall offered some privacy and, if Alex sat facing the wall, there was little chance of anyone overhearing—unless someone sat close to them, or he discovered Colbie's ruse and went ballistic. It was a chance she'd have to take if she wanted to get a glimpse through the window of what happened the weekend of the camping trip. As she waited, patrons darted in for the quick grab-and-go. No one paid attention to her, and Colbie wondered if they ever noticed anything—each seemed entrenched in his or her own world, completely disregarding any opportunity to interact with something other than technology—such as a human.

After picking up a tiny digital recorder that morning at a store specializing in surveillance, she carefully arranged it in her fanny pack, perching it on the table, zipper slightly open. The recorder cost a pretty penny, but it was instrumental in her search, and since she wouldn't take many notes during the interview, she had to rely on the stashed recorder to fill in any blanks. After each interview, she planned to listen to the recording, analyzing it as if she were back on the force. She was particularly interested in the voice inflection of each answer—her training taught her how to recognize stress by listening to the slightest nuances, and her intuition would come in handy since she could tune in on each person in the privacy of her own home. It was a good plan and, if everyone cooperated, she could tick down her suspect list in short order.

"Alex! Here!" Colbie motioned for him to join her, acting as if she were greeting an old friend.

"Hey! Sorry I'm late . . ."

"Not late enough for anyone to notice! Thanks for meeting me—have a seat . . ." Colbie guided Alex to the seat directly across from her—optimum for surreptitious recording.

"I really appreciate your meeting me today. As you know, I'm trying to piece together everything that happened before Brian disappeared. I know we talked before, but I don't have enough to continue my investigation." It was a good plan—by telling Alex she wasn't making much progress on the investigation, he would exhibit a subliminal reaction—relief. His body tell may be a brief sagging of his shoulders, or even an audible sigh. If he weren't involved in any way, there would be no reaction at all.

"Okay—how can I help?" No sagging shoulders.

"As I understand it, you went camping with Brian, Ryan, and two friends whom they hadn't met before. I'm kind of at a loss because I don't know those two guys, so if you can take me through the entire trip, I'll appreciate it. I know it's been nearly three weeks, but even the littlest thing might make a difference."

"Got it—okay—well, the trip really didn't have too many highlights. It was more of a weekend to get the hell away from everything. I remember Brian wasn't planning on going, and changed his mind at the last minute."

"Do you know why?" Alex paused, as if questioning whether he should tell Colbie what he knew. "Alex—you can tell me. You're not going to hurt my feelings."

"Brian mentioned you two weren't . . . in the best place, and he wanted to get away to think and clear his head. He didn't talk about it, though, when we were on the trip. In fact, he didn't talk to many of us, at all—he kind of kept to himself."

"Really? That doesn't sound like Brian—usually, he talks to anybody and everybody even when he goes through a rough patch."

"I know—weird, huh?"

"What about the two other guys—had Brian ever met them before?"

"I'm not sure, but I don't think so . . ."

"Okay . . . tell me about Kirk."

"Nice guy. Quiet. He and Vinnie seemed to be good friends, although I couldn't quite understand it."

"What do you mean?"

"Vinnie made snide comments about Kirk whenever he could . . . in fact, now that I think about it, Kirk seemed . . . whipped, if you know what I mean."

"Whipped? Really? I wonder why . . ."

"I don't know, but Vinnie is a strong, solid guy, and he seemed to like to tell us what to do—which might go along with what he does for a living."

"Which is . . ."

"He's some sort of outdoor guide, I think. Let me put it this way—Vinnie ain't small, and he ain't stupid!"

"Did you like him?"

"Me? No . . . not much."

"Did he and Brian seem to get along?"

"I guess—like I said, Brian was on the trip, but his reason for taking it wasn't for camaraderie, and we respected his privacy."

"Did Vinnie talk about anyone in his life? Friends? Girlfriend?"

"No, not really—the only thing I remember is his mentioning a guy he worked for."

"Name of the guy?"

"I don't know—it wasn't important to remember the name at the time."

"Did he mention what he did for a living?"

"Security, I think."

"Security? What kind of security?"

"I got the impression he was some sort of security guard."

Colbie sat back, absorbing what Alex just told her. This was a completely different take than she had before—she had no idea Vinnie was involved in security, or anything else that required him to carry a gun. *Then again, anyone who heads into the woods unarmed is an idiot. Brian probably took his .40 cal, too . . .* still, it was something.

"Do you know his last name?"

"Alberico . . . Vinnie Alberico. The only reason I remember is because I asked him about it. I hadn't heard it before, and he confirmed it's Italian."

Colbie turned the name on her tongue trying to jog her memory. Something didn't feel right. Something didn't track . . .

"Wait a minute—didn't you say he was an outdoor guide? He has two jobs?"

"I'm not sure—maybe the guiding thing is a weekend gig."

"Maybe . . ." Colbie couldn't take the chance that Alex would catch on to her recording, so she thought it best to cut the interview short, and move on. She watched Alex carefully throughout their conversation, and he gave no indication of dishonesty—her gut told her she could count on him anytime.

She checked her watch. "Good heavens, I'm late!" She hurriedly snatched the fanny pack and stood, offering Alex a bogus dismissal.

"I'm sorry, but I have an appointment at four forty-five—I can still make it if I leave now."

Alex grabbed his leather coat from the back of an empty chair. "Okay—I hoped this helped. I'm sorry I couldn't remember more . . ."

"Well, if you happen to recall anything else, will you call me? You have my number . . ."

"Yeah, sure . . ."

****

Colbie sat hunched at her kitchen table transcribing the notes from her conversation with Alex. It wasn't enough to hear them—she had to see them in writing to understand their full effect. Most of what Alex told her she already knew—but, the information about Vinnie Alberico? That piqued her interest. She closed her eyes to tune in—maybe something would come to her as she considered Alberico's possible connection to the case—at most, he would turn out to be the key for the lock and, at the least, his involvement would be nil. She considered the latter—she didn't think so. Colbie's gut told her Vinnie was involved somehow, and now it was time to investigate him just as she was investigating Remington.

What about Kirk? She concentrated on his name, requesting information from her intuitive being. Nothing. Nothing causing alarm, and nothing of interest. Alex's perception may have been correct—Kirk was a meek follower, incapable of harming anyone.

Vinnie was the one driving the bus.

11

Colbie sat cross-legged on her bed, sketching memories of her visions from the prior evening on her trusty yellow legal pad. To anyone else, they were chicken scratchings—to her, they embodied answers to all of her questions.

Each small 't' she drew was different from the others as she attempted to recreate the field of letters, none resembling the symbol she received while meditating. There was something about them not quite right, yet the longer she stared, the more she had no idea of what they meant. *I don't understand! What is it you want me to see? What do I need to know?* A dull headache took root as she lay back against the pillows and grabbed one of two books on her nightstand, flipping to a dog-eared page. Chapter Three. Reading was her therapy, really—without it she'd never get to sleep and, without sleep, she wouldn't be worth dirt in the morning. She slipped off her glasses, closed her eyes briefly to relieve mounting eyestrain, then focused on the page in front of her.

Without her specs the print was blurry, but she could see well enough to understand—Chapter Three, written out as two words, each word capitalized. She stared at the title and, in a second of serendipitous clarity, Colbie realized her mistake. *That's what I was doing wrong!* She traced the capital 'T' with her fingertip as she played the vision in her mind—*it's a capital 't!'* The capital 'T' in 'Three' had a downward stroke on each side of the t-bar, and the letters she drew had a cross stroke bisecting the t-bar. *Oh, my god! That's it! That's it!* Instantly, she recognized the significance of her error—the capital 't' resembled a hammer ride she often enjoyed at the county fair when she was a kid, but, she couldn't figure out what it had to do with her vision and the current situation—it seemed something to do with nothing. Yet, she trusted her intuitive mind to provide only true and valid information, so she couldn't go any further until she figured out what she needed to know.

By then it was a given that sleep was out of the question. Colbie logged on to the Internet searching images of hammer rides, thinking if she looked at pictures, something might jog her memory—or, provide further information about her reading. Photos of the popular carnival attraction popped onto the screen the second she clicked enter—some were double hammers, but it was the single hammer ride that interested her most. Two, conical-shaped compartments—enough room for four people, two on each side—positioned at the ends of a single long bar or beam, resembling jelly beans stuck on both ends of a toothpick. Still, she couldn't make a connection—*what does a hammer ride have to do with anything? I need more*! Her fingers clicked furiously on the laptop's keys.

A false dawn creeping through the bedroom window cued her promise to take a shower in ten minutes—if she didn't find anything by then, she'd have to wait until the evening to resume her search. She Googled anything resembling jelly beans on a toothpick, yielding little of interest—until she was ready to shut everything down. The last click on enter yielded images of oil jack pumps looking just like a jelly bean stuck on the end of a toothpick—like a hammer ride cut in half! In that moment, Colbie knew Ryan was right—the hammer ride and 't' in her vision corroborated Ryan's speculation that Remington's involvement in Brian's disappearance was predicated on untapped oil reserves. *This has to be it!* She wondered how irritated Ryan would be if she called him before sun up . . .

She dialed anyway.

"Ryan—Colbie. I know it's late—well, early—and I'm sorry. But, now I know without doubt that Nicole Remington is buying up the land because of hushed up oil reserves."

"How do you know that?" Ryan's voice was hoarse with sleep, sounding only mildly irritated.

"My vision—my vision!" Colbie recounted her story of her intuitive evening session, the hammer ride, and the capital 't.' "And, it wasn't until I saw a picture of an oil pump jack that it all made sense! You said it first, Ryan—you thought it might have something to do with oil reserves, and you were right!"

"Are you sure? You got all of that from a vision?"

"Yep—and, I learned a long time ago to trust my visions."

"This is weird—freakin' weird, if you ask me . . ."

"I know—but, for now, you're just going to have to take my word for it. Now, we need to find out everything we can about Remington's real estate deals—it shouldn't be too hard, since all transactions are public record."

Fifteen minutes later they said good night, each armed with important orders for that day. Ryan was to research real estate deals in adjacent counties brokered by Nicole Remington, and Colbie's responsibilities included an interview with Vinnie Alberico—if he consented to meet with her.

Her mind reeled with thoughts of Remington, her faceless accomplice, and someone named Al as she tried to get in a quick nap before beginning her day.

I'll figure it out, Brian—I promise! Just hang in there a little bit longer . . .

****

Remington snapped on the light, filling the room with a starkness revealing the worst in life. A sickening stench permeated slatted wood, and splintered fragments of glass lay on the floor, dull and without refraction, waiting to be swept into a better place. A floral couch jammed against the wall reeked of mildew and stale Doritos, a small end table made from a barrel standing staunchly by its side.

"Here's your dinner." Remington shoved a styrofoam to-go container at a figure sitting in a straight-backed chair centered in the middle of the room. "If you don't eat, it's your problem."

Brian raised his head to meet the eyes of his captor. "Thanks."

Remington removed the cuffs tethering him to the

chair, his wrists bruised and swollen.

“What day is it?” Brian calculated he had been there for over two weeks, but how much over he wasn’t sure.

“Thursday.”

Three weeks. He rubbed his wrists and hands as the cuffs came off, returning warmth and life into them. Up until then he spoke little to his captor, but perhaps now was the right time.

“You seem like a nice person,” he commented, wolfing down fried chicken and mashed potatoes. No gravy, and definitely not homemade. “Why are you doing this? What did I ever do to you?” His tone wasn’t accusatory—only questioning—a ploy he hoped would work.

“Shut up and eat,” Remington commanded, perching on a rickety stool by the door. Once attractive, in the dim light she morphed into something akin to a harpy or gargoyle standing sentinel at the threshold of its domain.

“I’m sorry—I didn’t mean to pry. But, are you okay? You seem a little . . . different.” Brian peered at her as if intently interested in her, not just what she had to say.

“What does that mean? I’m the same as I was yesterday, the day before, and the day before that—as if it’s any of your business.”

“I dunno—I guess I’m getting the feeling you’re being talked into this whole thing. You just don’t seem like a person who would do something like this . . .”

“You never met me before in your life—how do you know what kind of person I am?”

“You’re right—I don’t.” Brian paused. Even though he

didn't approve of Colbie's career choice as a profiler, he did manage to learn a thing or two from her days as an officer. She often talked about how to get a suspect to trust her and, in his present situation, he gained an appreciation for her gift to engage a subject as if she were a trusted member of the family. *I know you're looking for me, Colbie . . .*

Remington shifted her weight, studying the pathetic figure in front of her, thinking about his question. He was right—she wasn't the kind of person to treat someone horrifically. She wasn't a willing party to any of this, but what choice did she have?

"I'm sorry—I went too far. I didn't mean to get personal." Brian played his part to the hilt, catching Remington off guard with his apology.

"Forget it . . ." Without word she watched him. He didn't seem like a bad guy . . .

His only crime was living with Colbie Colleen.

****

There was just enough time to stop by the precinct before meeting with Kirk. She decided to talk to Kirk before trying to contact Vinnie, and he didn't sound any too thrilled about the prospect of having anything to do with her. But, Colbie made her best pitch and he finally agreed. If her assessment about Kirk's being a follower were accurate, she had to count on his being relatively weak in character. That was okay—just the way she wanted it. She was certain she could get to Vinnie through Kirk, but she had to plead her case as an overwrought girlfriend instead of an ex-cop. Intuition told her Kirk had a tendency toward the emotional, and appealing to him on that level may work. As with anything, it was a crapshoot—nonetheless, her progress over the last few days was significant and, for the first time in the investigation, Colbie felt rejuvenated and encouraged. Every day for the last three weeks, she mentally reached out to Brian with hope he would pick up on her search. Would he feel her trying to reach him? She hoped so—but, since he was so against her being a profiler and her abilities, she wasn't so sure.

She checked her watch as she pulled into a visitor's spot in front of the precinct's door. Ten-thirty. Her appointment with Kirk was at eleven-thirty, so the plan was to catch Sarge up on everything she learned within the past several days. She knew he wasn't making progress on Brian's disappearance since he hadn't contacted her, and although the murder investigation died down some in the press, it was ongoing. This meeting would be a quick in and out.

As she crammed notes in her purse, a large shadow appeared at the driver's side window.

"Well, well . . . if it ain't the fabulous Colbie Colleen!"

His tone was unmistakable, and Colbie knew it all too well—it was the one he used when intending to be cuttingly derisive and combative. She wasn't in the mood to deal with it—or, him.

"Alvin." She squinted up at him, her left hand shading her eyes. A faint whiff of cheap aftershave wafted in the partially opened window as he stood blocking her door, a gesture that was nothing less than subliminal bullying.

"I suppose you're here about your boyfriend . . ."

"Your business? I don't think so . . ." So much for the

feigned sincerity the last time she saw him. Colbie focused on stuffing the remaining notes in her bag.

"Any progress?"

"As a matter of fact, I'm making great progress!" She knew an upbeat tone would get under his skin, and she couldn't resist the opportunity when it so easily presented itself.

"Really? Great progress, huh? That's good . . . what did you find out?"

"Nothing I'm willing to discuss right now, but I fully intend on busting the investigation wide open soon."

"I might be able to help, you know—what do you want me to do?" His caustic tone turned calm and sincere.

"Really, Alvin, there's nothing you can do—but, I appreciate the offer." Colbie opened the door, pushing hard against his body. He gave way to the force, his face florid with anger.

"I have to go . . ." She locked the car, excusing herself without further conversation.

What a bitch, he thought as he watched her climb the steps.

What a bitch . . .

****

Colbie studied whom she assumed was Kirk get out of his car, and limp to the front door of the coffee shop. He stopped to read the flier Colbie placed on the front door weeks before, offering no clue or flicker of recognition. He was smaller than Colbie expected, reminding her of a piece of wheat ready for mowing—slender and blond, coupled with a look of ever-present uncertainty. Stick-straight hair brushed his eyebrows, his jaw and chin covered with a pathetic excuse for a beard. The limp threw her—neither Ryan nor Alex mentioned it, so she wondered if it happened after the camping trip. If so, what happened to cause such a pronounced, faulty gait?

Colbie waved from her table in the corner, standing as he approached, extending her hand.

"Kirk? It's nice to meet you—I'm Colbie." Kirk accepted the handshake, taking a seat in the recording chair directly across from her.

"I really appreciate your meeting me—I'm at the end of my rope, and I don't know where to turn. Truth is I don't know if you can help or not—but, it's worth a try." Colbie's voice caught, lending the perfect credibility to her performance. "I mean, I just don't get it? Why on earth would someone want to kidnap Brian?" She paused, waiting for his response.

"I don't think I'm going to be able to help you—I didn't know your boyfriend before the trip." Kirk leaned back, his fingertips flicking the side of his coffee cup.

"That's what I thought . . . so, what do you think happened?"

"What do you mean?"

"Well, the whole thing doesn't make sense. Did you have a feeling of anything being—amiss—during the trip? Did Brian seem weird to you?"

"Weird? No, not really."

Time for another tactic. Colbie's line of questioning was going nowhere fast. She took a sip of coffee, and sat back in her chair, her eyes misting with fabricated tears—a tactic she perfected prior to her police days.

She sighed. "I knew it would be a long shot—talking to you, I mean. But, you can't blame me for trying . . . I'm at my wits end, and I just don't know what to do."

Kirk shifted in his seat, uncomfortable with Colbie's emotions. He was always a sucker for tears, and he felt his eyes getting a little misty as he took a little too large of a gulp.

"So, what do you do? I know you can't tell me anything new, but we may as well finish our coffee, don't you think?" She lifted her cup as a toast, and took a sip.

"You mean for a living?"

"Yeah—are you doing what you love to do?"

He bit. "No, not really—but, I have to make a living doing something . . ."

"Why do you say that?"

"Well, security guard work isn't exactly the best job in the world. It's pretty damned boring if you want to know the truth . . ."

"Security guard, huh? Is it dangerous?"

Kirk laughed. "Dangerous? No—nothing ever happens. All I do is walk around and check doors . . ." Kirk's body relaxed, indicating he was feeling more at ease.

“Well, I guess it’s better than getting shot at!”

“True.”

“Where do you work?”

“Optimum Security—ever heard of it?”

“No—and, chances are I’ll probably never hear of it again!” Both laughed, lapsing into a momentary comfortable silence.

“It’s funny—Vinnie and I were just saying the other day how much we want to get out of there. The pay’s crap, and the guy who owns it . . . well, let’s just say I wouldn’t care if he disappeared.”

“Seriously? It’s that bad?”

“It’s not bad when we don’t have to see him, but when he’s around I try to make myself scarce.”

“That’s too bad—what a drag you have to put up with that at work. Is Vinnie the same Vinnie who went camping with you guys?” Colbie placed her cup carefully on the table, blotting her lips with a paper napkin.

“Yeah.” Kirk’s fingers tightened on the handle of his cup.

“I was thinking about contacting him, too—do you think he’ll talk to me?”

“Probably not.”

“Really—how come?”

“He doesn’t seem to give a crap about anyone or anything, so I doubt he’s too interested in your boyfriend’s going missing . . . maybe, but I doubt it. If he weren’t my boss, I wouldn't have anything to do with him."

Aha! There it is! New information—until then, she had no idea of where Kirk and Vinnie worked, let alone learning Vinnie was Kirk's direct supervisor.

"Why don't you quit?"

"I could, I suppose, but it's a drag having to look for a new job. Beside, I'm only killing time until I can start school."

"School? What kind of school?"

"Real estate . . ."

"Cool—I thought about buying a house once, but I didn't have enough for the down payment, so I decided to wait. Real estate is a good investment . . ." Colbie's voice trailed, her thoughts racing at warp speed.

"Same here—I should be able to start in the fall if everything goes according to plan."

"I don't know anything about real estate school, but I would think it's pretty expensive . . ."

"For me, it is."

"I know what you mean—everything costs a fortune these days!"

"It's tough making ends meet and save for school at the same time," he confessed. "But, at least the security gig has some perks . . ."

"Perks? Really? Like what?"

"Oh, nothing much—once in a while we have opportunities to work private detail, and those jobs usually pay pretty well."

"I bet!" Colbie glanced at her watch, employing the same technique she used with Alex. "Oh, my gosh—I have to get out of here! I have an appointment in thirty minutes!" She hopped up and grabbed the fanny pack, waiting for Kirk to take the hint.

"Thank you so much for meeting with me. Unfortunately, I didn't learn much—but, like I said, it was worth a shot.

"Yeah—no problem."

They parted as Colbie made an excuse of needing to make a call. Cell in hand, she sat on the street bench in front of the coffee shop, watching Kirk climb into his car. Her years as an accomplished interrogator paid off again—no one would ever know there was no one on the other end—only a ruse to buy time while Kirk drove out of sight. The fewer people who recognized her car, the better. She thought about their conversation, realizing there was one bit of information she didn't get.

Where the hell did he get that limp?

12

The meeting with Kirk didn't yield as much usable information about Vinnie as Colbie hoped—a disappointment because learning more about him was the reason for the meeting. All she knew now was he was Kirk's superior at Optimum Security, as well as the name of the owner.

Al.

Al? It can't possibly be the same Al, can it? Colbie flipped through tattered pages of notes searching for her initial insights about Vinnie, as well as her conversation with Ryan when he called her about seeing Remington at the restaurant. She recalled Ryan's telling her Remington called her dining partner by name, and she was certain the name was Al. But, as tired as she was, she knew she had to verify—it wasn't the time to rely on memory.

A third of the way down on the first page of the second tablet, there it was—circled three times, and punctuated with three exclamation points. She was right—Remington dined with someone named Al. But, was it the same Al who was the owner of Optimum Security? Could be. Investigating him and his business would be easy enough—a few clicks on Google, and she'd likely learn everything she needed to know. With luck, the company's website would have a picture of him, and she could have Ryan confirm it's the same guy. She weighed the possibilities—*if the same,* she figured, *he's probably in on Brian's kidnapping. If not, I'll need to investigate more.* Same old, same old.

She turned her attention to Vinnie—unlike Kirk, he may play hard to get if he were the loud, boisterous type Ryan described, or the tough guy Kirk described. Even if each were half right, getting Vinnie to talk with her might be difficult. From what she already knew, merely thinking of his name made her skin crawl with an uncomfortable darkness, and she was certain she wanted to meet with him in a public place.

He already gave her the creeps.

****

All in all, her investigation was going well, but working only with Ryan had its challenges. When Colbie was on the force, an officer always had her back and there was never a feeling of going it alone. Not so with her investigation—protecting her identity was critical, and without a few more bodies on the case there was a real possibility of blowing the whole thing. It was at times such as these extra bodies would come in handy.

Contacting Optimum Security was at the top her to-do list for the day, but she couldn't run the risk of her cell number registering on anyone's phone. Having someone run interference would be a plus, but, since that wasn't happening, she'd have to make the best of what she had. Earlier that day, she purchased a pay-as-you-go phone from a Wal-Mart on the other side of town—the number would show up on caller I.D., but her name would not. It allowed for the perfect anonymity needed to put the next step of her plan into effect and, if anyone called, she would answer as her alias—Kathy Simonson.

The phone screen illuminated her face as she tapped the keypad, laying bare the puffy dark skin under her eyes, her cheeks a bit more hollow than the previous week. Colbie never was one to primp, but she avoided mirrors more now than in the past. If Brian saw her, she wasn't sure he'd recognize her—ten pounds thinner, her normally pleasant face shaded with stress.

Three rings. "Thank you for calling Optimum Security—this is Tammy."

"Tammy, hi—my name is Kathy Simonson, I'm hoping you can help me, but I'm not sure who I need to talk to . . ."

"Well, do you need to hire a security guard?" The voice on the other end sounded sweet and willing to help anyone in need.

"I do—but, I'm not sure what I need. Is there someone I can talk to who can walk me through the process?" Playing someone who doesn't know much always works.

"Sure—I'll patch you through to Vinnie Alberico."

"Vinnie. Alberico? Interesting name . . . what's his position?"

"Operations Supervisor—he's been with us for a long

time, and he can tell you everything you need to know so you can find the perfect solution for your needs." The receptionist's tone changed to one of stark professionalism as soon as she uttered Alberico's name. *Is she part of it? No—why would she be?* Still, the thought nagged her.

"Perfect! Thank you!" *Bingo!* Colbie waited on hold for at least two minutes before the trained, professional voice interrupted her mental plan of attack.

"Mr. Alberico is on another call, but he shouldn't be long—do you want to hold?"

"Yes, please—I'm going out of town, so I'd like to get this off my plate, if possible!" Colbie tried to keep the conversation light, her comment meeting with ice.

"I understand—please hold."

As she waited, Colbie jotted down a quick list of questions to ask Alberico. Of course, she knew the answers to all of them, but she wanted to create a scenario of needing to hire Optimum Security for private detail, and it definitely wasn't the right time to look like an idiot. If he were on the take, her plan would offer the perfect opportunity to take advantage of her.

"This is Vinnie . . ." *Finally*!

"Mr. Alberico—thank you for taking my call. I'm short on time, so I'll get right to the point. My name is Kathy Simonson, and I'll be hosting a get-together for some very—influential—visitors. I'll need security detail for three days, and I'd like to hear about what Optimum Security offers. That is, assuming you can help me . . ." So much for the 'I don't know how to do anything routine'—her approach with Vinnie needed focus and force. It was time to drop the innocent thing—it got her where she needed to be, but now she needed to whet Mr. Alberico's appetite. Money wasn't an issue—at least he would think it wasn't.

"When you call me 'Mr. Alberico' I feel like an old man! Vinnie—my name is Vinnie."

"Vinnie—thank you. And, you certainly don't sound like an old man!" She laughed, figuring a little old-fashioned flirting wouldn't hurt a thing. She knew from Kirk that Vinnie was abrasive, so chances were good he enjoyed a little chest puffing every once in a while.

"So—tell me what you need." *Mid-to-late thirties,* she figured, assessing the timbre of his voice.

"In three weeks, I'm hosting a gathering for influential global investors—nothing big—just an intimate dinner for eight. Of course, a few will have their own security, but, for those who don't . . ."

"Got it. Where is the meeting?"

"I'm in the process of finalizing the arrangements—if I decide on Optimum Security, I'll provide the location in plenty of time."

"Do you anticipate any of your guests being in peril?"

Peril? An odd choice of words—an educated man? "Perhaps—these are high level real estate investors, and a few tend to be a little—ostentatious, if you know what I mean."

"I do, indeed!"

Trap set.

"Like I said, a few will have security guards with them—especially those from the Middle East. I'll need your best men . . ." There. The oil connection. If Alberico had a brain, he'd figure out real estate investors from the Middle East are interested in two things—oil and hotels. If he turns out to be brainless, he'd approach the job from the view point of a thug—a 'show me the money' mentality.

"Will you need grounds security, as well?"

"Probably not. I'm more interested in having your men inside keeping their eyes and ears open."

"Guest list? We'll need to have names so we can pull photos, backgrounds, etc."

"If I choose Optimum, I'll provide the list of names at the same time I send the location info."

"That's fine. I'm assuming since the event is in a few weeks, you'll be making your decision soon?"

"Of course—I'll be back in touch within two days. But, the thing we haven't addressed is cost—ballpark?"

"Normally, I could whip a number off from the top of my head—but, I'm thinking I should have a conversation with Optimum's owner, Al Vincent. He's hands-on, and I know your event will be important to him—and, he may have a couple of ways for you to save a few bucks compared to our competitors."

He wasn't a thug.

"Excellent! I'll call you tomorrow, late morning . . ."

Colbie bade a hurried goodbye before Alberico had time to ask for her phone number. If he were suspicious or interested, he'd ask the receptionist for the number registered on her caller I.D. *Will he call me back? Maybe. Or, will he try to investigate Kathy Simonson?* She didn't know—

either way, Colbie would gain answers to her questions. There was something about the way he conducted business that intrigued her. Clearly, he was no dummy . . .

Her gut told her he would call.

****

"I spent the day researching Tamlet County—it took longer than I thought, but some of what I learned is pretty interesting . . ." Ryan sounded tired, but not discouraged. That was good—Colbie could deal with a lack of sleep. Discouragement, however, was the first sign of an investigation spiraling into a cold case file.

"Cool—fill me in." Colbie grabbed her glass of wine, settling into Brian's favorite easy chair. It was her place of comfort, and it was easier to tune in on him when she could feel his energy.

"Okay—the first thing I found out was within the last five years, seven properties sold—Remington was the primary broker. When I researched the sales within the last twenty-five years there were only two up to the point when Remington started snatching up land . . . kind of tells me there was a reason someone was interested in buying seven chunks of land."

"I agree—do you know if the new owner changed the land in any way such as tearing down houses, or anything else that might indicate no interest in living on the property?"

"I don't know. But, I also found out none of those seven properties were listed—they sold on the down low, and they were quick, cash deals."

"Cash? That surprises me—do you think Remington has that kind of money?"

"Maybe. She's pretty high up on the real estate food chain . . ."

"True, but I'm guessing she has someone behind her pulling the necessary strings. Someone who knows how to get a deal done quickly, efficiently, and surreptitiously."

"Agreed. Are you ready for this? Remember the lady I talked to when we first began the investigation? The one with the dog? Well . . ." Ryan hesitated, as if preparing to deliver a powerful blow. "Remington tried to buy her property, but she couldn't get the deal done. The guy in the planning office said she was pissed about it, too—according to him, the woman didn't want to sell, and met Remington a couple of times with the double barreled at her side. Lassie, too."

Everything was beginning to make sense—oil reserves. Buying land. Keeping everything hush-hush. Colbie wasn't quite sure how to bring everything together, but one thing she did know—Remington was a pawn. But, why?

And, for whom?

****

Before she had a chance to pour a cup of coffee, the Wal-Mart phone vibrated on the kitchen counter. *Already?* She waited until the fourth ring, then picked up.

"Simonson."

"Kathy? This is Vinnie Alberico with Optimum Security."

Aha! "Good morning! What can I do for you?" No time for chit chat—if there were a point, he needed to get to it, her abrupt attitude signaling she meant business.

"Well, as we discussed yesterday, I wanted to speak with the owner . . ."

Colbie interrupted. "Al Vincent."

"Good memory! Al—that's right. Because of the caliber of guests for your dinner, he'd like to meet with you to make certain we present the best solution for your security needs."

Meet me? Curve ball.

"You know my schedule is full—I believe I mentioned yesterday . . ."

"I know—I remember you're on your way out of town. I respect your need for time, and I promise it won't take long."

Colbie paused, considering her options. She could refuse to meet him, and simply ask for a written quote submitted via email, or she could take a risk and agree to meet Al Vincent.

"I can't come to your office, but there's a coffee shop on First and Cross—what time?"

"Ten-thirty. Sharp."

"I can only give you thirty minutes—what does Mr.

Vincent look like?"

"About six feet. Greying hair. Big guy—solid build. You can't miss him . . ."

"Confirmed. I'll see you there at ten-thirty."

Colbie rang off, the possibilities of something going horrifically wrong playing in her mind. Finally, her investigation was ramping up, and she had the distinct feeling it was about to bust wide open.

Things were about to change.

13

Home away from home, Colbie thought as she placed the fanny pack on the table. With little traffic, she wound up with fifteen minutes to kill before meeting her mark. She positioned her chair for a clear view of the front door, making one last check to be sure the recorder was working. The shop was more crowded than last time, but there wasn't need for quiet as there was when meeting with Alex and Kirk. She pulled out her legal pad, still pristine and without notes. If she scribbled notes on a pad filled with investigation information, there was always a chance of prying eyes—a chance she couldn't take.

"Well, well—two times in one week! How did I get so lucky?"

Colbie cringed as Alvin pulled out a seat as if to sit down.

"What are you doing here? Shouldn't you be on duty?"

"Nope—not for another hour." He sat, knowing it

would piss her off.

"Don't get too comfortable—I was just leaving."

"C'mon—don't leave on my account!" Colbie gathered the fanny pack and tablet, scraping the chair on the floor as she pushed it back with her knees.

"Don't worry—I'm not . . ."

"Any news on the investigation?"

"Nothing since a couple of days ago." She slipped her coat on, fishing gloves from the right pocket. She had no intention of blabbing what she learned over the last forty-eight hours. "Don't get up . . ."

She turned her back on Alvin, and headed for the door. As much as she would have enjoyed seeing anger claim his face, she didn't want him to relish the satisfaction of the last word. Since her departure from the force, she attempted to treat her old adversary with respect, but she knew he wasn't worth it. He would always be a bully, never accepting the fact she promoted through the ranks because of her overall excellence.

She pushed on the heavy door, shifting her shoulder to give it extra force against a rising, stiff wind.

"Here—let me!" A man's voice sounded familiar. "You have your hands full!"

"I do! Thank you—I can't believe it's so windy!" Colbie lifted her head to get a good look at him for no reason other than it was the way she was trained. *Late thirties. Maybe forty.*

"Tomorrow, too, from what I hear!" He held the door for her as she braced against the wind's force.

Colbie thanked him again, and he disappeared into the coffee shop. *Do I know him?* A familiar feeling crept into her soul.

Something was wrong.

She didn't feel right about leaving before her meeting, but she couldn't risk Alvin's butting into her business. *Did he know I'm here? It doesn't make sense—he wasn't in uniform. Then again, his shift doesn't start for an hour.* Colbie stared at the front door. *He doesn't even live around here . . .*

What's he doing in my neighborhood?

****

"Vinnie Alberico, please."

Tammy's voice sounded tired. "He's out of the office until this late this afternoon. Would you like to leave a voicemail?"

"Please." No need to inform the receptionist of who she was—and, she didn't ask. Colbie still wasn't certain if the lovely Tammy had anything to do with anything. So, until she knew something concrete, Tammy didn't need to be reminded of the caller's false identity. Since leaving the coffee shop, Colbie questioned whether she made the right decision to call—dumping a connection or lead didn't make sense, so it was in her best interest to reach out to apologize for missing the meeting.

"Thank you." The receptionist clicked Colbie into

silence as she patched her through and, within moments, Alberico's voice greeted her with the usual prompt to leave a message at the tone. In that moment she realized why the voice of the man who held the door for her sounded so familiar.

It was Vinnie Alberico.

****

By six o'clock, Alberico still hadn't returned her call. There was a definite possibility of his being pissed about her not showing up for the meeting, but if he wanted to get a deal done it wasn't the best way to go about doing business. What bothered Colbie more, however, was her realization that the man who held the door for her at the coffee shop was Vinnie Alberico. When they made arrangements for her to meet Al Vincent, he said nothing of attending the meeting—if he were simply a go-between for Vincent, there was no reason for him to tag along. If, however, he were something more—elevated—then he had a personal stake in the possible security contract. Something wasn't making sense—something that may clear up with a quick phone call to Ryan.

He answered immediately. "Hey! What's up?"

"Just trying to figure out a few things—remember when you saw Remington and someone named Al at the restaurant?"

"Of course—why?"

"Well, when I went over my notes, I didn't get a solid

description of what the guy looked like . . ."

"I didn't get to see how tall he was, but he was pretty solid—he probably works out would be my guess."

"How old?"

"About forty-five. Not young, but not old."

"What color was his hair?"

"Greying, but it looked like it was on last stages of red."

"Red? You're certain?"

"Pretty sure—he looked Irish, or something close to it."

"That's what I thought, but I wanted to make sure."

"Why? Do you think you know him?"

"Maybe. I have to put a few pieces together, but let me put it this way—it's all starting to make sense. I'll fill you in, but I have to sort out a few things—I think I'm on the right track. Back at you later . . ." Without saying goodbye, Colbie ended the call.

One more to go.

"Sarge? Colbie. I have an odd question for you—what's Alvin MacGregor's middle name? I wracked my brain, but for the life of me, I can't remember . . ." Colbie counted on Sarge's being busy, not having time to talk to her about Brian's case, or why she wanted to know Alvin's middle name.

"His middle name? Geez—I'm not sure, but something tells me it's Vincent."

“Vincent! That’s right! Thanks—I owe you one!”

“What does . . .”

“I promise—I’ll tell you later!” She clicked off, holding the phone against her chin, thinking about what she just discovered—the missing link.

Al Vincent was Alvin Vincent MacGregor.

14

Something was bugging her. Colbie still couldn't believe Al Vincent was Alvin MacGregor, her nemesis at the precinct for over a decade. None of it made sense—why would Alvin live a dual life? Why was he involved with Nicole Remington? Most important, why would he kidnap her boyfriend? There was always the possibility she was making a mistake, but she didn't think so—the pieces fit, leaving coincidence a distant second.

It was well into three weeks since Brian's disappearance and, from everything she learned so far, it made sense the kidnappers needed him alive—always subject to change, of course. The revelations of the past couple of days began to fill in a few gaps, but a thorough review of every note Colbie scribbled since the beginning of her investigation would make certain she was connecting the dots—the right dots. With Alvin in the mix, what seemed inconsequential then may be of import now.

The time for organization had long since come and

gone, legal pads stashed in every room. Knowing her propensity for writing down ideas and notes wherever she happened to be, she rifled through her car receipts, napkins, or anything else that could accept a pencil or pen—even a gum wrapper. *Man—I need a better system!* she thought as she stuffed her pockets with bits of paper. Twenty minutes later, her kitchen table was scattered with legal tablets, tiny note pads, sticky notes, and miscellaneous stuff.

She was ready to dig in.

Nothing caught her eye until she reached the part of the investigation including Nicole Remington. Her review reminded her she first saw Remington in the parking lot driving the green Subie—some of the questions she scribbled had answers, others were no longer germane. Then there was the brownstone—for the first time, she knew exactly where Remington lived, her apartment number, and the names of each owner or tenant—*Brownburg, Jamison, Carson, Marshall, Vincent, and Remington,* she recalled.

Colbie picked up the small top-spiraled notepad, adjusting her glasses to make sure she was reading her notes correctly. Vincent? She couldn't believe it! Why hadn't she noticed that before? Her blood pressure spiked as she realized the significance of her find—Alvin lived in the same brownstone as Nicole Remington under the last name of Vincent, his real middle name. Now, there were more questions than answers, and she had to rearrange the puzzle pieces to include a scenario she hadn't considered.

This wasn't about Brian—it was about her.

****

"I know . . . I can't believe it, either. I never would have thought—ever—that Alvin MacGregor was involved in any of this. But, everything points in that direction, and I don't think there's any way we can ignore it." Colbie got Ryan on the line as soon as she was certain MacGregor was a critical element of the investigation. His reaction was the same as hers, and both asked the same question—what the hell does MacGregor have to gain?

"Do you remember when I told you the guy in the restaurant looked familiar? Now I know why—I used to see MacGregor on the streets as he went from business to business, checking on things. I guess that would be when he was a beat cop . . . "

"Good idea, but, as far as I know, Alvin was never a beat cop—always squad with a partner."

"Why does that make a difference?"

"Because at the precinct there was a distinct separation between the cops who walked the streets, and the guys who patrolled the streets with a bigger territory. Their paths would cross once in a while, but not often. How many times did you see him?" One or two times wouldn't be of much interest—more than that would be and, if that were the case, Colbie had a hunch as to why.

"Oh, man—several times. Always around the same time, too. I had a standing meeting on Friday afternoons with a particular client, and I was there every week for about five months. I'll bet I saw him twenty times—maybe more."

"Twenty? Are you sure?

"Pretty sure—I just can't believe I didn't put two and two together when I saw him in the restaurant."

"How many years ago did you see him every week?"

"Mmmm—five. That was the summer when it was so stinkin' hot . . ."

"I remember—do you recall when Remington first showed her face around here? I think that was in your research . . ."

"Holy shit! You're right—I think it was around that time. I'll check to be sure, and get back with you to make certain we're understanding the same thing. And, I think we are . . ." Ryan's respect for Colbie inched higher each time they talked for her ability to dissect and understand was incredible, and he soon realized he could learn a lot from her.

"I think we understand it just fine. Now, we have to concentrate on why Alvin kidnapped Brian—in fact, Brian doesn't have anything to do with it other than he's involved with me."

"You? What?"

"Think about it—three weeks ago, I told you enough for you to know Alvin hated my guts when I was at the precinct. I tried to avoid him, but, when he was on my team, he was nothing but trouble. He attempted to destroy my reputation and, when that didn't work, he became absolutely unbearable."

"Geez—nice guy."

"Make no mistake, Ryan—Alvin MacGregor is a formidable foe. His involvement takes this investigation to a whole new level—a dangerous level."

"You have a plan, I suppose . . ."

"Kind of—if Alvin is after me for some reason, we have to make sense of what Remington has to do with any of this."

"Any ideas?"

"One—I need to find out why MacGregor was visiting businesses as if he were a beat cop. I have an idea, but it involves serious allegations and I damned well better be able to prove them."

"Like . . ."

"What if MacGregor is on the take?"

"You mean like a Shylock or protection racket?"

"Pretty much—but, more on the money end. What if he's playing a mafia game, and businesses have to pay up each week? Every Friday."

Ryan whistled as he realized the implications of Colbie's thinking. She was right—this was big and, when brought to light, it could bring down more than MacGregor and Remington. The whole damned precinct would be under the microscope.

After ringing off with Ryan, Colbie sat back, hands hooked behind her head, considering her next move. Before ending the conversation with Ryan, she picked his brain about the names of businesses where he saw MacGregor each week, all in a part of town she didn't know well—she'd have to be careful not to ruffle any nerves. If she went poking around and pissed someone off . . . well, it could mean trouble for her as well as curtains for the investigation. And, who's to say MacGregor was still involved with the con—if it were a con.

She fired up the laptop, deftly entering the names of the businesses, one by one. It was doubtful many of them would have websites given the area of town, but it was worth a shot. Ryan indicated there were seven businesses, in all—two restaurants, a dry cleaner and laundry, one grocery market, one mahjong parlor, and a liquor store—all on one block. Her research of the area showed the area held a strong Asian component in the center of a fifteen-block area while other cultures conducted business as well as lived on the fringes.

Even though she were an ex-cop, it was a good idea to bring a friend along for back up—and, if she could swing it, she'd ask one of the cops at the precinct who had contacts in that area. One problem, though—Sarge was never going to believe her. He'd certainly stick up for one of his officers until he had irrefutable evidence that targeted allegations were true—not until. Colbie supposed it would be easier if she didn't have such a soft spot for Sarge—this was the kind of thing that would not only piss him off, it would offend him personally, and she didn't relish being the person to burst his bubble about one of his own.

By the time she got ready for bed, she whittled the scenario down to a couple possibilities—the first seemed far-fetched, but, up to then, nothing about Brian's case was normal, so it was worth considering. What if MacGregor were a crooked cop with a long history of strong arming uneducated business owners into paying a fee for his looking the other way when it came to criminal acts? The far-fetched part wasn't about the criminal acts—it was more about his being a dirty cop. Of course, such things happened all the time in other cities, but they didn't happen in her town. In her precinct. If, in fact, Alvin were dirty, were other cops in on it? A real possibility. If this scenario were correct, what was now a mess would turn into an absolute debacle the second the press got wind of it. When she thought about it, her first-case scenario was probably the easiest to figure out. On the surface it seemed cut and dried, but there had to be a lot bubbling beneath the surface—however, once everything started to deteriorate for the parties involved, the situation should come to fruition quickly. The second, though, wasn't such a clear shot.

Optimum Security.

For Colbie, it was a hornets' nest in the making. For all of her years on the force, she never heard of Alvin's having a second career let alone a different life. The first thing she needed was an answer to the question of how long he was at the helm of the security firm. The second was a list of the company's clients—next to impossible without the help of someone on the inside.

Perhaps the lovely Tammy . . .

****

The following morning, Colbie checked with one of her buddies on the force to see when Alvin was scheduled to work. She didn't want to take any chances of running in to him—not because he was a total ass, but because he was a suspect. She didn't need him poking his nose where it didn't belong and, besides, she needed more than drop-in time with Rifkin. For this, she needed to schedule time with him, possibly away from the precinct if he could swing it.

According to her contact, MacGregor was off on Thursdays and Fridays—same days off for years—and, when she questioned her friend, she learned Alvin rarely showed up at the precinct on his days off. What didn't track, though, was Ryan's saying MacGregor was in uniform when he saw him on each of those Fridays. Or, did he? She flipped through her notes, double checking her recollection of the conversation. No, Ryan didn't say he was in uniform, but he certainly implied it—the uniform was the main reason he noticed Alvin at the businesses in the first place.

When she got down to it, Colbie recognized there were at least two different investigations balled into one. Foremost was Brian—where they were holding him, and why they were holding him. Unfortunately, to figure those two things out, she had to get to the bottom of the crap she just learned about MacGregor and Alberico. If someone didn't spill his guts soon, all bets were off.

Colbie needed an informant.

15

Two candles leapt to life, casting dancing shadows across Nicole's face. What may have been attractive and enticing at one time turned ugly and contorted as candlelight revealed hollowing cheeks, as well as a complexion turned sallow and ashen. No, time wasn't being kind to Nicole Remington—it was kicking her ass.

Her fingers lingered on napkins as she lay them on the small bistro table by the bay window. *How the hell did I get myself into this mess*? she wondered. *It used to be so easy—I could handle things. Now? If I'm not careful, I'll wind up in freakin' jail*... One thing she knew for sure—she had to find a way out. She didn't know how or when, but her evening with Alvin was a start. If she told him she wanted to end their relationship—completely sever it—there would be hell to pay. She was in so deep, she often wondered if she would wind up in a ditch somewhere, body broken and unrecognizable. Oh, she wasn't being dramatic—it was a real possibility. The truth was she was afraid of Al Vincent, and if she didn't tow the line, well . . .

Since moving into the brownstone, Vincent had his eye on her. Whether his interest were for more personal reasons, she didn't know—but, since he was the owner of the building, she figured it a good idea to be cheerful and inviting. So, at the beginning of their relationship, things were pretty good—Vincent treated her with respect, always praising her success as a well-respected business woman in upper crust real estate circles. Five years ago, they were a good fit, and Remington thought he was the one.

My, how things change.

The day finally came when Vincent made his move over dinner, dropping the bombshell that he knew all about her nefarious real estate deals—and, if she didn't comply with his requests, she'd be up the river in no time. He made it clear he had no intention of making their relationship legit because he only needed her for two things—snapping up real estate in an oil-laden region, and an occasional tryst. That's it. Nothing emotional. Nothing at all. What she didn't understand then was Al Vincent's dual life—she didn't have a clue he was a cop. She didn't know about Optimum. She never saw his apartment in the building because he always visited her, so his living in a different location didn't occur to her. Why would it? She regretted not vetting him during the neophyte stages of their relationship—partnership, if she wanted to get technical. If she had, she might not be in such a mess.

It also didn't occur to her he used an alias.

To Remington, Alvin MacGregor didn't exist. She knew him as a rich owner of a classy brownstone, dripping money. At first, they occasionally dined out and, when they did, he always kept a wad of cash rolled up in his pocket. He didn't mind flashing it, either—she liked that. And, savvy real estate broker she was, there was always the possibility he may want to sell the brownstone. What better way to secure a contract? Truth was they were using each other, both of them knew it, yet each refused to admit it to the other. Whenever she asked him about how he knew of her felonious activities, he said it was none of her business. She finally quit asking because what he knew about her was true—knowing his source was moot.

It was then her career transformed into something she barely recognized. For the last five years, she researched and purchased real estate—cash—where there were untapped oil reserves, all under Vincent's direction. He provided leads and money, and it was her job to persuade landowners to take it and run. Make no mistake—it was a lot of bucks. Vincent always believed money talks, and he knew if he offered a new life to many who didn't have enough money to buy a loaf of bread, they'd jump at the chance. He was right, too—some deals were like slicing through room temp butter. What he didn't count on was a ridiculous, emotional attachment to land—many owners didn't want to sell because their property had been in the family for generations—a bullshit reason, according to Vincent.

The raucous call of the buzzer yanked Remington to reality—it was now or never. It was time to lay her groundwork carefully, and raising suspicion about her wanting out would derail any possibility that ever happening. At the second buzz, she checked her make-up in the hall mirror before opening the door, disappointed in the reflection. There was a new sadness in her eyes and, as she answered a second buzz, she wondered if it were too late.

She hesitated before opening the door. "Hey, Baby . . ." Al insisted she use the term of endearment, although she wasn't sure why. She considered it an intimate greeting, yet he managed to turn it into something dark and unappealing. Vincent brushed past her, dropping his keys on the library table under the mirror.

"Smells good. What's for dinner?"

"Roasted chicken—it'll be done in about twenty minutes. Wine?" Remington plucked two wine goblets from her grandmother's antique hutch, offering both in a toast as she grabbed a bottle of merlot.

"Red wine with chicken? What do you have that's white?"

"Chard—good?"

"Fine. It's a hell of a lot better than merlot . . ." Vincent muttered, his comment laced with obvious distaste, his bullying always an undercurrent. But Remington couldn't take any chances at ruining the first stage of her plan, so she went along with his disrespect for there was more to gain by compliance. Besides, doing so bought a bit of time, allowing the wine to do its job. It wasn't a ploy to impair his senses—only to relax him a bit. Anything more, and he would certainly blame her for his inebriation.

They settled into plush leather armchairs, facing each other, the fireplace turned on for ambiance. When Remington bought the flat it had a wood-burning fireplace, but she couldn't be bothered with actually ordering wood. Within a week of taking possession, the new gas version was in place, adding false comfort to a life about to spin out of control.

"I'm thinking of selling . . ."

"This? You're thinking of selling this?" Over his dead

body.

"Yes—I haven't decided for sure, but I think I need to be somewhere warmer. Maybe the southwest . . ." Remington presented her idea with a soft voice, glancing at Vincent over the rim of her glass. "Will you come?"

"With you? Are you serious?" Vincent's florid complexion turned deep crimson at the mere suggestion of her leaving.

"Maybe. I don't know. All I know is I feel as if I need a change, and I'm hoping we can move—maybe carry on what we're doing somewhere else." First twist—run the same game only in a different place? It was possible, and Remington knew it would appeal to him.

"You're serious . . ." More a statement than a question. He shifted in his chair and crossed his legs, placing more weight on his left hip. He resembled a caricature of an English lord, ascot and all. *Good—his body didn't tense*, she noted.

"Tell me more . . ." The idea of moving the operation wasn't a bad one—Remington didn't know anything about Optimum, but he could operate the company from anywhere. Of course, he would demand Alberico move with him. Tammy? He wasn't sure—she was good for ordering around, and she was great with customers, but there was always the nagging question of her being not too bright. Even though she presented herself as a professional, truth was she was a high school graduate who somehow managed her way into a cream-puff job—good pay for doing her job and keeping her mouth shut.

"Look—if we stay here, it's a fact our luck will run out," Remington continued."Why wait until then? Isn't there somewhere that will provide us the same opportunity? There has to be oil just waiting to be sucked from the ground . . ."

"Maybe. I can check it out."

"Well, how did you find out about the oil here?"

Vincent wasn't comfortable sharing particulars with Remington. It was none of her business about anything—her job was to negotiate real estate deals, and close her yap.

"I know a guy . . ."

"Contact him, then—see if he can help us find new territory!"

He was quiet as he drained his glass. "It's something to think about—but, it won't be as easy as you hope it will be."

"Why? What do you mean?"

"I'll have to think about it." He looked at Remington, trying to decide if she were on the up and up. She could be up to something, but she wasn't bright enough to put one over on him. He knew it, and she knew it. So, maybe her suggestion had merit. Maybe not. But what about his career as a cop? Letting go of that weakened his position in more ways than one—for starters, he would lose considerable income in the Asian district. He might also lose income by relocating Optimum Security, although he knew he could easily build it up again. The real crapshoot was Colbie Colleen . . .

He wasn't done with her yet.

16

Colbie listened again to her professor's lecture on willful blindness as she flipped through her tablets, extrapolating and combining each note about Nicole Remington. Even though she knew them by heart, she wanted to see them in front of her to make certain she wasn't missing something. Doing so ensured her investigation didn't dilute due to lack of cohesion—it was something Sarge taught during her first weeks on the force. Her vision of the blindfolds made perfect sense and, when coupled with her police and psychology training, they added up to the same thing—where there's smoke, there's fire. Of one thing, she was certain—it was time to confront Nicole Remington, yet something told her she needed to tread carefully, almost as if family relations were at stake.

A face-to-face could end up a bust, but Colbie doubted it. Her gut told her Remington was business savvy, but when it came to a personal life, things weren't so rosy—if she came down too hard on her with a bad cop routine, it probably wouldn't play well. No, as with Alex and Kirk, her best bet was to meet her somewhere neutral yet more concealing than a coffee shop. A place with low-light. More secretive. If she met with Remington in the evening, it was likely she would be tired and, perhaps, more prone to letting down her emotional guard. Even so, it would be a tricky conversation to balance, and it all boiled down to discovery. Her psych and police training ingrained when the mind is curious and seeking something such as deception, it tends to pop off the page—of course, it was there all the time obscured by a willingness not to see. Not to recognize. But, by casting aside willful blindfolds, clarity is always the inevitable result. Since her professor's lecture, Colbie incorporated his training into her investigation, and it were as if the room exploded in brilliant light. She couldn't dispel the benefits of removing her personal blindfolds, and she was ready to continue pursuing Brian's kidnapping with each of her senses ready to receive the most subliminal information. The notes in front of her were concrete, but it was time to let her intuition guide the investigation without distraction.

It was time to turn herself over completely to what she already knew.

She pieced her notes together as she would a puzzle, each according to chronological time frame. Remington's name was always in the wings waiting for Colbie to recognize its significance as it pertained to each aspect of the investigation, and she was certain Al Vincent held Remington emotionally hostage. It was up to her to break through on a level she knew instinctively would force Remington's emotional dam to break.

She took a deep breath and tapped in Remington's office number, preparing to be patched into voicemail.

"Elite Real Estate—this is Alison."

"Good morning, Alison—Nicole Remington, please."

"Please hold."

The receptionist clicked off, offering Colbie the opportunity to listen to a litany of real estate properties on the market. Within seconds, a low-slung voice greeted her.

"Good morning—this is Nicole Remington." Her voice was deeper than Colbie expected, and surprisingly sultry.

"Ms. Remington, my name is Colbie Colleen . . ." Colbie listened, opening her senses to everything she heard on the other end of the line before words—a short gasp, then silence. She continued. "I'm certain you know who I am, and why I'm contacting you."

Remington paused, uncertain of the appropriate response. "Yes . . ." Her voice was barely a whisper.

Colbie paused for effect, allowing her intuition to guide her. Because she entered the conversation without expectation, she recognized Remington's single-worded answer was tinged with resignation.

"It's over, Ms. Remington. As it stands now, you're in a heap of trouble—but, something tells me you're not acting in your own interests. Am I right?"

"Yes . . ." Again, her voice was barely audible.

Colbie tuned into Remington, her mind's eye revealing the symbol of a hamster in a cage with a wheel. The vision corroborated it was the right time to back her suspect into a corner—right then, Remington was trapped, and she knew it. Any attempt to disengage, and she would simply be spinning her wheels.

"Look—I want to help you, but I need you to help me.

How about if we meet this evening at Conlan's Steak House at eight-thirty? Conlan's was perfect—it hadn't changed since the '50s, and Colbie considered it one of the gems of their city—quiet, and out of the way. "Do you know it?"

"I do. I'll meet you there at eight-thirty." Remington sounded like a small child in trouble for leaving the back door open.

"Excellent. I'm certain if we work together, we can achieve what needs to be done." Colbie rang off, confident in Remington's showing up. *She has a lot to lose,* she thought. *She'll give up Vincent . . .*

****

The steakhouse was just as Colbie remembered it. She hadn't been there for about ten years, but it looked exactly the same—as she entered, red faux-leather booths lined the walls on each side, small tables positioned in the middle. Its smell was familiar—grilled steak lightly scented with mildew. It took a second for her eyes to adjust to the dimmed light as she scanned the restaurant for Remington, but she hadn't arrived. A woman of about sixty welcomed her, hand poised gracefully on the menus atop the hostess stand. As did the restaurant, the hostess appeared stuck in time, her hair stacked in a greying beehive.

"How many?" she asked.

"Two please—a booth in the back, perhaps." The woman nodded, leading Colbie to a private booth perfect for a confidential meeting. She slid in to the middle of its curve as the hostess laid two menus on the edge of the table. "I'm waiting for someone—she's tall, dark hair with a red streak, in her mid-thirties . . ." There was no need to say more. The woman nodded her understanding, and offered to send the cocktail waitress over to take her drink order. *Not tonight*, Colbie thought as she opened a menu. *I need to have a clear mind . . .*

She focused on the front of the restaurant so she could assess Remington's body language and posture as she entered. Colbie was confident once her suspect made it to the table, Remington would adopt a defense posture, and she wanted to study her before she steeled herself for an accusatory onslaught. Remington had no idea of what to expect from their meeting—all she knew was she was on the hot seat, and it behooved her to expect the worst.

Five minutes later, Nicole Remington pulled open the heavy wooden door, appearing timid and unsure. Gone was the glitz and glam of the woman filled with confidence Colbie saw walking up the steps of the brownstone only a few weeks previous. Instead, Colbie witnessed a woman whose soul was owned by someone else, her thirty-five years long passed believability. Her hair was one color, the playful cherry streaks replaced with something more conservative, and she appeared shorter than Colbie remembered—then again, compared to her own diminutive frame, anyone seemed taller than she.

Pretending to look at the menu, Colbie analyzed Remington's demeanor as she spoke with the hostess. No smile. Not a flicker of personality. As she approached the table, she stayed behind the hostess by three or four paces—almost as if she were afraid to get any closer. As if she were exceeding her station in life. *Abuse*? Colbie wondered. *If so, at the hands of Al Vincent?*

"Here she is!" The hostess smiled widely, revealing a

row of cigarette-stained teeth.

Colbie returned the smile, extending her hand to Remington. "Right on time! Thank you for being so prompt!" No use in making her feel worse—besides, the plan was to act as a caring friend. She could tell by looking at Remington she didn't have far to go to reach her breaking point—and, the way things were going to go, she'd probably reach it that night. Remington accepted the handshake and slipped off her coat, folding it meticulously before draping it over the back of the booth—a quick assessment told Colbie it was cashmere. High class, and pricey.

Remington hesitated, realizing her first predicament of the evening. Because Colbie seated herself squarely in the middle, Remington had no option—no matter how she positioned herself, she would be sitting next to Colbie, not across from her. It also forced her to turn at an angle to face her accuser—both of which Colbie planned. By facing Colbie, it automatically placed Remington in a more relaxed position. Colbie planned to mirror her, giving the appearance to anyone not knowing better they were old friends catching up over dinner.

"Do you mind if I call you Nicole?" Colbie asked as Remington slid into the booth. She chose to sit to Colbie's left, turning her body to the right as she tried to get comfortable. Slightly pulled back, her head tilted to the right, indicating an immediate uncertain, defensive posture.

"That's fine . . ."

"Good. Something to drink?"

Nicole shook her head. "No, thank you—water is fine." Colbie listened carefully to the nuances of her speech—

the word ‘fine’ preceded by a slight hesitation. *Everything sure as hell isn’t fine*, she thought, as Remington shifted uncomfortably in the booth.

“Okay—I think I’ll order an iced tea. That sounds good . . .” She signaled the server then looked Remington in the eye.

“Shall we begin?”

****

Within the hour, Colbie knew for certain what she suspected—Al Vincent pulled all the strings. Remington spilled her guts about everything, including her less-than-above board real estate deals complete with Vincent’s blackmailing her.

“I don’t know how he knows, but he does . . .” Her eyes filled with tears as she realized Al Vincent played her for a fool. “I’m an idiot . . .”

“No—you’re not an idiot. There isn’t anyone alive who hasn’t made some pretty serious mistakes, so you can’t beat yourself up about it.” Colbie felt a pang of guilt as she watched her once adversary crumble before her. Still, she possessed one more bit of information that would probably send Remington around the bend—Al Vincent was really Alvin MacGregor.

And, he was a cop.

Colbie considered revealing her trump card, but just because Remington was emotional and weak, her fractured spirit didn’t mean Colbie could trust her. She had to keep in mind Vincent molded her easily, and Colbie's guessed his talons were long, always in a death grip.

By the time they were ready to leave, Colbie had enough information to bring Vincent to his knees, but timing remained an issue. As she suspected, Remington was only a part Alvin's overall scheme, but it did come as a surprise she already started to change the balance of their relationship. Remington confided in Colbie she could no longer stand the sight of him, and if it weren't for her being in so deep, she would have kicked him to the curb long ago. It was also a surprise that Remington came clean so fast—but, all that did was solidify her suspicion that Nicole Remington didn't have what it takes to fight back, and she let Vincent get the best of her.

Colbie also decided to hold back the info about Vincent's being a dirty cop—armed with that knowledge, Remington might pull back thinking her life were at risk. Although she didn't come right out and say, Nicole Remington was scared witless of Al Vincent, and it was clear to Colbie there was abuse in Nicole's life. Whether it were inflicted by Vincent remained a question, but Colbie instinctively knew he was at the crux of everything.

As they spoke that evening, Colbie searched for outward signs indicating the abuse was physical, but there were none. Remington wore a tasteful long-sleeved blouse, pencil skirt, and knee-high boots, so it was hard to tell. But, when Colbie opened her mind to Remington as a whole, it was obvious the scars were emotional. Perhaps a little slapping thrown in, but such actions didn't appear to be the root of her fear. Remington was quick to let Colbie know jail didn't appeal to her, and she would do anything to save her own skin. That admission provided Colbie the necessary leverage she need to take down Vincent, and she wouldn't hesitate to use it when the time was right.

Until then, she needed to keep Remington close.

Before calling it a night, Colbie wanted to know one thing—was Brian still alive? She felt he was, but she was so close to the investigation she had to be certain. In the moment of asking her question, Colbie felt buried emotions surge, her eyes brimming with tears. She wasn't proud of it—no self-respecting cop would be caught doing such a thing. But, in reality, she wasn't a cop anymore, and letting Remington see her pain wasn't a bad thing—she counted on its cementing their partnership to bring Al Vincent down, and it seemed to work, too—Remington patted her hand as she confided Brian was just fine.

Then she dropped the bombshell that Vincent was after her, not her lover.

Just as Colbie thought.

****

Colbie sat in her car in front of the restaurant, trying to absorb what Remington disclosed—Al Vincent was targeting her for whatever reason. When she pressed Nicole about why he had her in his sights, Remington said she didn't know. That made sense—because Remington didn't know Al was a cop, she wouldn't have any idea as to Colbie's and Alvin's checkered professional history. No wonder he didn't want to tell her how he knew about her murky real estate deals—it had to be through his time at the precinct.

As pissed as she was, Colbie had to think calmly and clearly. Part of her wanted to bust into Sarge's office ready to do battle with Alvin, while another part—the biggest—wanted to nail him so he couldn't take advantage of any loopholes. He was smarter than Colbie thought, and in order to send him up for the rest of his life, she needed more.

She needed proof.

She closed her eyes, and leaned back against the headrest—a migraine jockeyed for position as she realized for the first time in her investigation she was drained. Brian's disappearance was bigger than she imagined and, in one evening, it transformed from a kidnapping only to kidnapping, fraud, and police corruption.

The only good news was learning Brian was fine. Remington promised Colbie she would make certain he was treated as well as possible without arousing Vincent's suspicion. As far as she knew, he didn't have plans other than to make Colbie sweat—and, according to Remington, he enjoyed every second of it. *Of course, he did,* Colbie thought as she recalled her last encounters with Vincent—*because he's Alvin MacGregor.* He always asked about the investigation as if he were interested in Brian's welfare—and, hers. She knew better, but couldn't see the truth because she wasn't looking for it. At least, what she perceived to be the truth. Now, blindfolds removed, she looked squarely in the face of evil, understanding the complex reality of her situation. Alvin's hatred for her twisted the investigation into skewed angles, and she needed to make sense of them.

Colbie opened her eyes as the owners of the restaurant were closing up shop. *I need to get some sleep,* she thought as she backed the car out of the parking space. *I'm going to need it . . .*

Intuition told her things were going to get worse before

they got better.

She sat in the car for a few more minutes, trying to gain understanding of the task in front of her. She had the chops to bust things wide open, but she had to be careful—tangling with Alvin MacGregor was worse than walking into a hornet's nest.

17

Colbie brought Ryan up to speed the following morning, then dialed Optimum Security—she was certain Tammy would be interested in what she had to say. The familiar voice greeted her, and Colbie lost no time in getting to the point.

"Tammy, my name is Colbie Colleen, and I'd like to take you to lunch today. Is twelve-thirty a good time?"

"I'm afraid I don't know . . ." The receptionist struggled to maintain her poise.

"You're right—you don't know who I am, so why should you have lunch with me? Well, for this reason—I'm investigating some—interesting—business practices at Optimum Security, and I need to find out if you're involved." Colbie knew in order for Tammy to take her seriously, she had to make her think she was involved in something illegal. She may or may not be, but Colbie really didn't care about that. Chances were pretty good Tammy was merely a pawn, and she couldn't do much for the investigation other than secure confidential information and hand it over.

"Me? How can I be involved in anything? I don't even know what you're talking about!" Tammy's voice reached an annoying squeak as she realized the possible ramifications of what Colbie just told her. *Maybe she's not that stupid,* Colbie thought as she listened to the rising fear in the receptionist's voice.

"Well, that's what I need to find out—I'll meet you at the restaurant across from Optimum Security at twelve-thirty. Until then, I suggest you keep our conversation to ourselves . . ."

"But . . ."

"Tammy—really? I assure you, you're not in a position to argue. I'm investigating serious allegations and, if you want to keep yourself out of what is already a giant mess, I suggest you suck it up, and meet me. Now, I can help you—that doesn't mean I'll have the same offer two weeks down the road."

That did it. Tammy quickly agreed.

Colbie ended the conversation with Tammy's promise she wouldn't open her mouth. But, as with everything else in the investigation, Colbie couldn't trust anyone or anything. Contacting Tammy was a risk she needed to take, and she didn't want much from Tammy other than a list of clients and personnel—anything else would be a gift.

Calls accomplished, she set out for the south side of town to investigate the possibility of Alvin MacGregor's being on the take. She tried to get one of her officer friends from the precinct to go with her, but no one was available. Not the best situation, she had to move forward to an area of town with which she had little experience, but its reputation suggested it was a good idea to go packing. She wished she could slip back into the comfort of her uniform—at least it would afford her some sort of protection. Now? No one would care who she was, or why she was there. She could disappear as easily as her boyfriend and no one, other than Ryan, would have a clue about where to look. The only other people who gave a rat's ass about the investigation—Brian's parents and sister—were completely worthless, and Colbie couldn't trust them to remember her last name. No, she was on her own as she parked in front of the dry cleaner's.

The pungent smell of chemicals mingling with steam greeted her as she pulled open the metal barred glass door. A small rack of freshly pressed shirts stood next to the cash register, and the phone rang raucously until a small Asian woman scurried in from the back room of the shop. Inconspicuously, Colbie listened to the phone conversation with little hope of understanding anything—the woman spoke Chinese.

She nodded to Colbie as she hung up.

"May I help you?" Her accent was thick, and Colbie needed to listen carefully to understand her correctly.

She smiled. "I hope so—I want to talk to someone about the cop who visits you each Friday." She wasn't sure how the woman would react—as with many foreign cultures, when someone comes knocking asking about something other than dirty shirts, English becomes a non-existent language. This time, she got lucky—the woman appeared to understand her, and Colbie detected a slight look of alarm flicker in the woman's eyes.

"You wait here," she commanded as she disappeared between two cheap cotton curtains. Within moments she returned, accompanied by a middle-aged man who was most likely her husband.

"How may I help?" The man refused Colbie's extended hand.

"Well, I'm not sure—but, I'm hoping you will speak to me about the cop who comes here every Friday." She paused, studying his response.

"No one comes here . . ."

"Really? Do you mean he doesn't come here now?" The man nodded, and she knew it was a lie.

"Did he come here before?" A nod.

"How long ago?" The man was silent, unsure of what he should say. Colbie sensed an element of fear and, knowing Alvin, she was certain he threatened the man standing before her. "Did he threaten you?" Silence. She tried again. "How long ago was he here?"

The man looked at the floor, then at his wife. "Last week."

"Does he come every week?"

"He come every Friday for last five years. He tell me if I say anything, he hurt me and my family . . ."

Colbie cringed as the man's posture slumped as if expecting the worst because of his telling the truth.

"Does he take money from you?"

"Yes."

"How much?"

"Two hundred dollar . . ."

"Every week? Does he have the same arrangement with other businesses on this block?"

"Five—five businesses. Every week."

"Do you know if he collects the same amount of money from them?

"I don't know. We say nothing."

"I understand. Has the policeman ever hurt you?"

"No."

"What does he look like?"

"Big. Orange hair." Immediately Colbie knew he was talking about Alvin—his hair was the type of red that was more like bright copper than anything.

After a few more questions Colbie thanked them, leaving the couple standing behind the register, watching her as she walked out the door. Certain she was out of sight, the man picked up the phone, and dialed.

****

The restaurant was packed, and Colbie had to wait for a table. She preferred something a little more private, but wound up smack dab in the middle of the restaurant floor. It wasn't the best choice—if Tammy decided to lose it, there could be an uncomfortable scene, but it was another risk she would have to take.

She did, however, have an excellent view of the Optimum Security building from her table. At precisely twelve-thirty-five, Tammy made her way across the busy street, checking her watch as she stepped onto the curb. *She looks nervous,* Colbie thought as she watched her check her cell—a fleeting smile as she read what Colbie guessed was a text message. In that moment, Colbie knew—she felt—Tammy was, indeed, a pawn. A brief image of a chessboard popped into her mind's eye, large fingers removing each piece slowly and methodically. She watched as the fingers lingered over the queen, then flicked it off the board in swift, dismissive motion. Two pieces remained—the king and one pawn.

"Are you Colbie Colleen?" The vision dissipated at the sound of Tammy's voice.

"I am. Please—have a seat." Colbie gestured to the seat across from her, but Tammy pulled out the chair to Colbie's right. *Interesting—she chose to be closer to me rather than far away,* she noted as Tammy hooked her shoulder bag over the back of an empty chair. It was an important tell—by choosing to sit next to Colbie, Tammy indicated she was a friendly person, and she didn't perceive Colbie as a threat. She felt comfortable with her. Odd, because that's exactly what Colbie didn't want to happen. *Maybe I misread her—maybe she doesn't know anything.*

Tammy's body language convinced Colbie to change her tactic at the last minute. "I appreciate your meeting me—I know I came across pretty strong on the phone, but I'm concerned for your welfare . . ."

"My welfare? What does that mean?" Tammy pulled her head back, shifting her weight to the opposite side.

"Well—let me ask you this . . . how well do you know

the people you're working for?"

"You mean Vinnie?"

"Yes—Vinnie, and everyone else—how well do you know them?"

"Not well—why?"

"Because there are some things—illegal things—going on with Optimum Security. I can't go into the particulars, but I need your help . . ."

"My help? How can I help you?"

"I need a list of Optimum Security clients, as well as all employees."

"Are you kidding? If I get caught, I'll get fired! I have a three-year old kid to support!"

Learning Tammy had a child caught Colbie off guard. "Let me put it this way—if you don't help me, you won't have a job anyway. Not to mention, if you don't help me, there's a real possibility you'll go down with the ship." Colbie looked directly at Tammy with a stone-faced look.

"But, I haven't done anything!" Tammy's eyes welled with tears.

"Unfortunately, I don't know that—however, you might be able to convince me . . . tell me what you know about Optimum Security. Not the stuff the public hears—I want to know what happens when no one is listening." Colbie watched as Tammy came to a slow understanding that she had to play ball. Tammy straightened in her chair, looking directly at Colbie.

"Let's start with Vinnie Alberico . . ."

18

Colbie gave serious thought about how she would broach the subject of Alvin's corruption with Sarge. She really didn't have concrete proof—only suspicion—and it would be the first thing he would call to her attention. He and Alvin were friends simply based on Alvin's number of years on the force, and Colbie was clear Sarge would jump to his officer's defense at the mere suggestion of corruption. She couldn't blame him for his loyalty, no matter how misguided, for it was the way of the officer community. They treated each other as family, and there would be no shortage of colleagues who would step up for him. The question was would they step up for Alvin even if they knew the truth? And, perhaps, the bigger question—would they step up for her?

She made a note to call Sarge before the end of his shift to schedule an appointment and, in the meantime, she would comb over her conversation with Tammy. By the time they left the restaurant, Colbie had no doubt Tammy was a chess piece in the Optimum Security game—she didn't know anything, but when Colbie pointed out she or her family may be in danger, Tammy was quick to cough up whatever information she had—information she didn't know she had until Colbie adroitly extracted it. She also promised Colbie she would have a list of clients to her by the end of the day, and Colbie had to give her credit for recognizing she was in a situation over which she had no control. Would Al Vincent or Vinnie Alberico harm her or her family? Chances were against it, but Colbie couldn't take chances with anyone's life—especially a three-year old child.

It turned out Tammy was quite the fountain of knowledge when it came to Vinnie. When Optimum hired her, she was fresh out of college—no business experience except a brief stint at a law office. That job was okay, but when she saw the ad for the opening at Optimum Security, she jumped at the chance. Colbie asked her the starting salary, stunned when Tammy confided it was sixty thousand a year. *For a receptionist who really isn't very bright?* It sounded fishy, but since she didn't have any idea of what a receptionist should make, it was something she could quickly research. Still, the inflated salary lent credence to Colbie's suspicion that Optimum Security was up to no good.

Around three o'clock, Colbie called Ryan to fill him in on what she learned that day. Her time spent at the dry cleaner's and lunch with Tammy was the most interesting since Ryan didn't have anything concrete for her.

"It was clear they're scared witless of Alvin," she commented after recounting her morning on the south side of town. "And, I wouldn't put it past them to tip him off. They seemed to know the other businesses Alvin strong arms, so it makes me wonder if they have a network of business owners who keep their eyes peeled for something unusual—or, someone unusual. Like me."

"It's always a possibility," Ryan agreed. "Even from a distance, Alvin seems like an imposing guy."

"He is—and, he's as nasty as the day is long. I'm going to have to be careful, and gear up the eyes in the back of my head when I visit the station within the next day or two. Which brings me to my next point—I tried to get in touch with Sarge, but he wasn't in. Another case, I'm guessing . . ."

"How do you think he's going to take your suggesting his officer is dirty?"

"Are you kidding me? He's going to be pissed, and he'll probably take it out on me. He'll want to see the evidence."

"And, right now, you don't have evidence . . ."

"True. That's why I can't wait to get my hands on the list of clients and employees of Optimum—Tammy has access to Vinnie's office, and she knows the password to his computer."

"What? How did she swing that?"

"I don't know, and I didn't ask. She's going to meet me at five-thirty—after what I told her today, she's scared to send anything from her work or personal email."

"Can't say I blame her—if I worked for those guys, I wouldn't trust them, either."

"I know—I feel like I'm getting her in a crapload of trouble, but what choice do I have? I have to find Brian, and I have to find out why Alvin is targeting me. Somehow, Optimum is involved—I just don't know how." Colbie paused, thinking about the trouble she brought into

Tammy's world.

"What about Brian? Do you know exactly where he is?"

"Remington told me they move him around—at first, they had him in the house on the outskirts of town. The one you investigated—you know, where the crazy lady with the dog lived . . ."

"Why didn't Remington tell you about the other places? You know damned well they're keeping him in an empty house on her realty radar."

"That's what I think, too. She assured me Brian is fine, and Alvin has no plans to take things further—but, I don't trust him and, loose cannon that he is, he may change his mind. But, as far as her not telling me where the houses on rotation are, I think it's because she doesn't quite trust me, and she really doesn't trust Alvin. Remember, she still doesn't know he's a cop . . ."

"Are you going to tell her?"

"I'm not sure—I may be able to get around it by upending the Optimum thing. I have to see the client list first . . ."

Colbie and Ryan chatted and brainstormed for another half hour before Colbie realized she had to meet Tammy at the coffee shop. She hoped the information the receptionist was providing would unlock much of what she didn't know. Yes, it was a crapshoot, but, right then, it was all she had to figure out the Optimum Security component of her investigation.

As she waited for Tammy, she thought about what the receptionist told her about Vinnie Alberico. When she first hired on at Optimum, he put the moves on her within the first couple of days. At first he seemed nice, but after she got to know him a little better within the office environment, he gave her the creeps. Tammy felt he had a mean streak a mile wide and, when Colbie pressed her as to why, she confided Vinnie forced himself on her in the parking lot one night when they stayed late at work.

Tammy's confession about the sexual assault didn't surprise Colbie in the least. Her body language at their first meeting was similar to Remington's in that both hunched their shoulders forward, heads slightly down—classic postures for registering defeat. Psychology and police training taught her such postures were often referred to as 'the turtle effect,' and they're seen in those who are humbled or lacking confidence. Tammy, however, exhibited more pacifying behavior by stroking her décolletage when she spoke of Alberico's unwanted advances. Subconsciously covering her neck indicated to Colbie that Tammy was experiencing emotional discomfort, fear, or concerns right then. *Why wouldn't she be stressed,* she thought as she swirled sweetener into her tea. Between Alberico and the news she may be in legal hot water, Tammy had plenty on her plate.

Colbie glanced up as the receptionist approached her table.

"Sorry I'm late—traffic was terrible!"

"No problem—how did it go?"

Tammy slipped into the chair across from Colbie, unaware of the recorder in the fanny pack on the table. She pushed it aside, making room for three manila folders.

"This is all I could get . . ." she commented, shoving the folders across the table to Colbie. "You'll see right away which files come from Vinnie's office . . ."

"Why do you say that?"

"Because some of them don't make sense."

"What do you mean?"

"Well, when I looked through them, I noticed his transactions don't match the transaction's I have in my files."

"Why do you keep track of transactions, at all?" Colbie thought it interesting that Alberico and the higher ups trusted a receptionist with sensitive material.

"Because they're one girl short—Vinnie doesn't have an assistant anymore, and I had to work on the files."

"Why are they short-staffed?"

"The girl who left didn't tell me, but I could tell she was scared of something . . ."

"Alberico?"

"Probably . . ."

Colbie sat back and sipped her tea, thinking about what Tammy just told her. She hadn't considered Alberico's being a serial rapist, but it did make sense—Alvin could have come across Alberico in his cop years, tagging him to be just what he needed. Someone who needed to make a deal . . .

"What's her name?"

"Kellie Marchand—I wrote her phone number on the inside of the file folder." She paused. "There's one other thing . . ." Tammy's teaser roused Colbie from her thoughts.

Colbie raised her eyebrows, and put down her cup. “What’s that?”

“Someone—I have no idea who it is—calls to speak with Al or Vinnie every Friday.”

“Do you know about what?”

“No—but it’s at the same time every week, and Al or Vinnie are always there to take his call. He says his name is Jim, but I’m not sure I buy it.”

“Really—why not?” It made sense that Al Vincent would be at the Optimum office on Fridays, one of his days off at the precinct.

“I can’t really say why—something just doesn’t feel right.” With that statement, Colbie renewed her trust and faith in the Optimum Security receptionist. Tammy had her eyes open wider than Colbie initially thought, and Colbie was beginning to think she could be of great benefit to her.

If she’s game, Colbie thought. *If she’s game . . .*

****

By six o’clock, Colbie was back at home, the files Tammy left with her on the kitchen table. Her Mr. Coffee was on its last legs, spitting water as she fired it up for a full pot—combing through each piece of paper was going to take time, and she needed to be as alert as possible.

While the coffee brewed, she separated the folders—two were from Alberico’s files, one was from Tammy’s desk.

Excellent! She copied them! After spending time with her, Colbie recognized Tammy wasn't a dummy, and she was no one's fool—she made copies so she wouldn't raise suspicion should Alberico or Vincent go thumbing through the files. Handing Colbie originals could have been the kiss of death for her, as well as Colbie's investigation.

Sifting through Alberico's file, she pulled out pages with the same or similar information in Tammy's file. First up, Optimum Security's client list—without looking at its contents, Colbie noticed Alberico's list was two pages, and Tammy's was one. The info was identical on the first page, but the second page included a list of handwritten names. It was possible, she supposed, the second page was simply missing from Tammy's file—then again, it would be interesting to find out if Alberico added it himself.

She dialed Tammy's personal cell from the Wal-Mart phone. Several rings later, she was about to hang up when Tammy answered, sounding out of breath.

"Tammy—it's Colbie. Do you have a sec?"

"Uh, not really." Colbie instantly tuned into the stress in the receptionist's voice.

"Tammy . . . is everything okay?" Colbie paused, listening intently to the subliminal tells.

"Yeah—sure. My boss just stopped by, so I really don't have time to talk."

Colbie picked up on her signal immediately. "Alberico is there?"

"Right. Do you mind if I call you later? I don't want to keep him waiting."

"Do you want me to call the police?"

Tammy's voice caught as she answered Colbie's question. "No—that's okay. I really gotta go . . ." End of call.

Holy crap! Why is Alberico at Tammy's? What could he possibly want?

Colbie could think of only one thing.

****

She led Brian, blindfolded, through the back door, and instantly he knew he was at the first house. It reeked of stale urine and mildew and, if he listened carefully, he could hear fearful scurrying of an occasional field mouse.

It took his eyes a minute to adjust when Remington removed the blindfold—scuff marks on the dusty floor were still visible, so not much changed since he was last there. After a while, days began to merge into each other, but he counted four moves within the last two weeks. Remington was always the taxi service, although he was well aware someone else was involved.

He still didn't know why.

Remington stood in front of him. "What I'm about to tell you—well, you need to keep your mouth shut. Understand?"

What the hell is she talking about? Remington barely spoke to him whenever she was there, so why would she talk to him now?

"I know you don't know why you're being held here

and, to be honest, neither do I. All I can say is you probably don't have any reason to worry—your girlfriend is looking for you."

Colbie? How does she know about her? Brian struggled to comprehend what he just heard.

"Did you talk to her?" He looked up at Remington, trying to decipher any emotion on her face. The irony wasn't lost on him—he was doing exactly what Colbie was training to do for her career.

"I did more than that. All you need to know, for now, is things will probably start to move quickly."

"What does that mean?"

"I said enough . . ." Remington didn't want to let too much out of the bag for fear of compromising Colbie's investigation, as well as fearing Al's discovering her duplicity. She was counting on Colbie to take Al Vincent down—only then could she rest easily.

Brian had to take advantage of Remington's loose lips. "One more thing—and, I won't say a word—who's behind this? I know as sure as I sit here this isn't your idea. Am I right?"

Remington hesitated, wondering if she were saying too much. Although she couldn't imagine how Al Vincent would learn she was selling him out, she also never imagined herself in such a position in the first place.

"Keep thinking . . ."

That was all she said.

19

Colbie found herself thinking about her last call to Tammy. She hadn't heard from her since then, and she began to question whether she made the right decision. She didn't want to come across as a mother-hen type, but she did worry something happened. She didn't trust Vinnie Alberico as far as she could throw him—even so, it wasn't any of her business, and Tammy was perfectly capable of taking care of herself. She hoped. The problem was her intuition was telling her otherwise—and, it wasn't until she thought about her professor's lecture on willful blindness that she made a decision.

She dialed Tammy's number.

Several rings later, voicemail took over. Tammy's voice sounded young, and Colbie thought how difficult it must be to have the responsibility of caring for a young child. Since she didn't want to come off as a Nosy Nettie, she left a generic message asking her to call as soon as possible. That was all she could do—but, if she didn't hear from her by the following day, she'd investigate further. In the meantime, she had plenty to keep her busy.

****

Ryan parked across the street from the dry cleaners, under a tree providing decent cover. His car looked like others on the street, so it was likely no one would notice as he surveilled the block. He had the perfect vantage point to see across the street and up, but he had no view of those businesses on the right side of the street. He'd have to change his position if he wanted to surveil them, as well.

It was a long time since he visited the south side—five years when he thought about it—but everything looked the same. In fact, nothing changed—still loaded with culture, along with dark alleys that made his skin crawl. The area had its difficulties, and it was widely known to outsiders as a rough part of the city. Those same outsiders also thought no one in their right mind would walk its streets after dusk—but, with an escalating crime rate, it was the perfect feeding ground for a money hungry, dirty cop.

He remembered Alvin showed up around noon, giving him ten minutes to adjust the settings on his camera. He scooted over to the passenger's side to avoid detection—the last thing he needed was someone calling the cops on him. That way, he was in the shadows and his telephoto lens would do the heavy work. The tree provided the shade he needed to camouflage himself, plus he wore a dark navy hoodie to further blend into the interior of the car.

Ryan thought it odd there weren't more people on the streets. For a Friday it was nearly deserted, and the only person he saw was half a block away. All he had to look at were some poorly designed storefronts—until a red-haired cop turned the corner, heading directly for the dry cleaners. *Bingo*! *And, he's in uniform*, Ryan thought as he snapped pics of Alvin's pulling open the door—Ryan's telephoto lens was brand new, allowing him perfect, close-up access.

Three minutes later, Alvin strode through the door, making his way up the block. Same thing—disappear through a door, only to leave minutes later. Four times. Even without knowing how much Alvin was extorting from the business owners, it had to be a tidy, weekly sum. Within fifteen minutes Alvin disappeared, rounding a corner. *Probably stashed his car*, Ryan surmised as he watched him walk out of view.

He texted Colbie to let her know he got the photos, and they agreed to meet later that afternoon. She had no idea what time she would wrap up her end of the investigation, so they settled on touching base around five o'clock.

Right then, she was more concerned about Tammy.

****

Colbie timed her call to Sarge for late afternoon, right before the end of his shift—it was the best time to find him in his office and, if everything went according to plan, he would spend a little more time with her on the phone. The past several times she spoke with him, he was rushed due to a backlog of cases—this time, she had more to present and she wanted to get his thoughts on the whole Optimum Security thing. Certainly he would be interested, but she still had to tell him the news about Alvin. Colbie wasn't sure if she wanted to drop that bombshell right then—she wanted physical evidence of wrongdoing and, until then, Sarge wouldn't give credence to her theories—whatever they were. Until she sifted through all the information Tammy provided, she wouldn't have a complete picture. She did have a couple of questions about the files, though, so they served as the perfect excuse to check on her.

Tammy picked up on the fourth ring.

"Hi, Tammy—it's Colbie. How are you doing?"

"Fine . . ." Her voice sounded strange, as if she were talking with a mouthful of rocks.

"Are you okay?" Colbie listened carefully to her voice, noting any differences from Tammy's regular tone and inflection.

"Yeah—I'm fine."

Colbie didn't buy it. Mental alarms were in full swing, and she knew something was wrong. Very wrong. She also knew Tammy wouldn't tell her—so, time for another approach. With Colbie doing most of the talking, Tammy answered questions about the files.

"Okay—that's it for me." Colbie paused as if she were trying to remember something. "Oh, one more thing—what's your address?"

"My address? Why do you need it?"

Colbie avoided the question. "Don't worry—I'm not going to use it against you. I'm just trying to keep all of my notes up to date—I don't want to take a chance on getting confused!" Her reason didn't make much sense, but Colbie counted on Tammy's not really listening.

"Oh. Okay. 1579 Charleston Place."

"Got it! I'll call again if I need anything else . . ." With that, Colbie ended the call before Tammy had a chance to say a word.

Propped up against the kitchen counter, Colbie cupped her hands around her oversized cup of tea, thinking about Tammy. *She sounded weird,* she thought as she replayed the conversation in her mind. *I don't know what, but something is wrong.* She couldn't think about it any longer—grabbing her notes and keys from the kitchen table, she was out the door.

She knew Tammy's area of town, but she didn't know it well. Initially, she thought Tammy lived in an apartment, but was pleased to see the address was a cute bungalow set back from the street. She parked at the curb in front of the picket-fence gate, sitting for a moment to see if there were activity in either the yard, or outside. *At least her son has a yard to play in,* she noted as she scanned the neighborhood. It was too quiet—the cop in her told her something wasn't right—so did her intuition.

The cement walkway was cracked with bits of grass growing in its jagged seams, and the front door needed a good coat of paint—other than that, it appeared to be in good shape. The neighborhood was established with the majority of residents in their forties and up. Tammy's living there appeared an anomaly, but it seemed a good environment for her child.

She rapped on the wooden door, listening carefully for the slightest sound. Nothing. She knocked again.

Tammy slowly opened the door, the late afternoon

sun highlighting the right side of her face. Colbie stared, stunned, at the woman standing before her—Tammy's face, beaten and blue, was swollen to the point of her right eye being completely shut. She held an ice pack to her lower right jaw, droplets of water streaking down her forearm.

"Holy shit! What the hell happened to you?" Colbie opened the door, inviting herself inside. "Did Alberico do this?"

Tammy nodded.

"When? The day I called you?" Colbie led her into better light so she could see the extent of her injuries. She tilted Tammy's head slightly to the left, her fingertips gently resting under her chin. The bruising exploded under her jaw, snaking up the side of her face.

"Where's your child?" Colbie glanced around the room as she asked the question.

"He's staying with my sister."

"Did he see you like this?" Tammy nodded.

"Did he see Alberico wail on you?"

The receptionist's eyes filled with tears. "Yes . . ."

"Did you go to the hospital? Did he rape you?"

Tammy shook her head. "No—he got pissed when I wouldn't give him what he wanted."

Colbie asked again, "Did you go to the hospital?"

"No—I'll be okay." Her response was classic. So many abused women don't want to get treatment or report an assault and, to Colbie's way of thinking, it was a foolish decision although she understood it. Tammy undoubtedly knew if she went to the hospital they may report the incident to the cops.

It wasn't a secret Vinnie Alberico threatened Tammy with further harm if she opened her mouth. He was the type who thought he could take whatever he wanted and, until then, it may have been true. But, what Colbie also realized was his beating Tammy to a bloody pulp would be his undoing—it was the open door she needed for her to ask Sarge to pull him in for questioning.

She planned to do exactly that.

****

"It probably wasn't the best idea to order Chinese chicken wings," Colbie commented as she wiped her fingers on a paper towel. "They're too damned messy!"

Ryan laughed as he reached for another. "They may be messy, but they're good!"

She sat back in her chair, looking at Ryan. His account of Alvin's coming and goings on the south side were interesting, and she was thrilled he snapped photos. She slipped the thumb drive into the port of her laptop and, a couple of clicks later she was looking at fifty pictures of Alvin from the time he entered the dry cleaners to when he rounded the corner at the far end of the block.

"He's so stinkin' arrogant—he doesn't have a clue we're surveilling him. He can't imagine anyone would . . ." The more she looked at him in the photos, the more she was beginning to hate his guts.

“Yeah—I made sure I was as inconspicuous as possible. He was in each business for only a couple of minutes, then it was out the door to the next.”

Colbie enlarged each picture enough so she had a good look without compromising pixilation.

“Ryan! Check this out . . .” Colbie adjusted her glasses, leaned forward, and squinted at the photograph on her screen.

“Hold on a sec . . .” He wiped off his fingers while Colbie slid the laptop to an angle so both of them could see.

“Look—right there!” She pulled the picture to full screen, pointing to Alvin’s left front pants pocket. “It didn’t look like that when he went in . . .” She compared the pictures side-by-side. “I’ll bet that’s a wad of money! Makes sense, too—the business probably doesn’t have a bunch of large bills hanging around, so the owner probably paid Alvin in smaller bills. Tens. Twenties—maybe smaller.”

Ryan leaned closer to get a better look. “You’re right—I bet he has a stash of cash rolled up in his pocket!”

The picture of Alvin leaving the dry cleaners was the only one providing a good front view of his body. As they reviewed the other photos, by the time Alvin completed his rounds, both pant pockets were bulging considerably.

“Excellent work! This is the proof I need so I can take it to Sarge—now he can do something, and I’m going to ask him to start with Vinnie Alberico.” She looked at Ryan as she took a swig of coffee. “If I tell him about Alvin now, I’m not sure how he’ll handle it—but I’m thinking he’ll want to do his own investigation into Alvin’s second—no, third—job. Optimum Security is his second. Fleecing timid business owners is his third. However, no matter how I look at it, Sarge won't immediately do anything—he'll want to be sure first . . ."

"What if he refuses to do anything at all?"

"He can't if we have proof of one of his own helping himself to citizens' money."

"Well, maybe . . . but something tells me it isn't going to be quite that easy."

"You're probably right, but I have to start somewhere. I'll call him in the morning to set up a time to talk—I want to be sure Alvin isn't anywhere near the precinct."

"Smart . . . good luck!" Ryan pushed his chair back, and grabbed his jacket. "Let me know how it goes . . ."

****

Even though is was Saturday, Colbie had a fifty-fifty chance of contacting Sarge at the precinct. The murder case from a few weeks ago was still active, so every cop he could spare was putting in overtime, including him. She sat on her couch, laptop positioned just right, considering what she would say. If she decided to bring up Alvin, she had to walk on eggshells when presenting her suspicions for she was certain Sarge wouldn't take it well.

She dialed the precinct, asking the cop on the front desk to patch her through.

"Sure thing—he just got here."

Colbie thanked him, and waited for Sarge to pick up.

"Rifkin."

"Sarge! It's Colbie—I'm glad I caught you!"

"I just walked in the door—what can I do for you? Any news on Brian?" He paused for a moment before continuing. "I'm sorry we haven't been able to put as much time into it—the Lansing murder has all of us working extra hours."

"I know—I'm keeping up with it when I watch the news. Although, I have to admit, I haven't had much time to do that."

"So—what's up? Why are you calling?"

Colbie swallowed hard. "Well, I do have news about Brian's case—any chance you have time to meet with me this afternoon?"

"This afternoon? I don't know if . . ."

"I'll be brief, I promise—I won't take up much of your time."

Sarge paused, considering whether he wanted to meet with her after his shift. "Come in at four—I only have half an hour, though—Melissa and I have plans for this evening."

"You got it—I'll be there at four!" Colbie clicked off, considering her good luck. *Maybe*, she thought, *just maybe this is the break I need*!

****

At precisely four o'clock, Colbie waited for Sarge outside of his office. Clements was on the desk when she arrived, and he informed her Sarge would be back within fifteen minutes—she could wait, but there was a possibility Sarge may be later than that.

"Thanks, Clements—I think I'll wait." She headed down the corridor, running into only two officers by the time she reached Sarge's office. She knew Alvin wouldn't be there—he hadn't shown up on a Saturday since her time at the precinct, so there was no likely reason for him to start.

It was twenty minutes before Sarge ambled down the hall.

"Hey, Colbie—c'mon in . . ." He flashed his toothy smile as he greeted her. *Must've had a good day,* she thought as she gathered her stuff from the chair beside her. He opened his office door, standing aside so she could enter first.

"Have a seat . . ." Sarge plopped several folders on his desk, then headed to a small refrigerator he kept in the corner to grab a bottle of water. "So, what's the news?" He sat down at his desk, leaning back in the old- fashioned precinct chair.

"My investigation is going pretty well, and I've made progress, but—I'm not quite ready to bring my findings to you, yet."

Sarge raised an eyebrow. "I don't get it—then why are you here?"

Colbie recounted her visit to Optimum Security, leaving out the part about running into Alvin at the coffee shop. For this conversation, she decided she didn't want to mention Alvin's name at all. Thirty minutes later, she paused to take a breath, leaving the weight of what she told Sarge hanging in the air. She told him everything. Tammy. Alberico. The attempted rape.

"The thing is, Sarge—I think Alberico is up to his neck in Brian's disappearance, but I don't have any proof. If you haul him in for questioning regarding Tammy's attempted rape, maybe he'll slip and say something about Brian. He will, at least, be a blip on your radar . . ."

Sarge sat silently before commenting. "Did Tammy file a report?"

"No—she's too scared."

"I should have a report to get this going, and I'll need to talk with her. But, since the murder investigation is winding down, I can put a couple of guys on it."

Colbie breathed an audible sigh of relief. "Thanks, Sarge, I really appreciate it." She hoisted her messenger bag over her shoulder as she prepared to leave. "Will you let me know when you bring Alberico in for questioning? I know I can't be here for it, but I'll appreciate an update."

"You got it . . ."

As Colbie walked across the parking lot, something didn't feel right. Sarge didn't exhibit his usual disgust when talking about Alberico's smacking Tammy around. She recalled several years ago when a victim showed up at the station to file an assault report, Sarge was Gung ho for nabbing the S.O.B. who did it. When Colbie told him about Vinnie Alberico assaulting Tammy, it almost seemed as if he feigned interest. *What's up with that*, she wondered as she climbed in behind the wheel.

She eased out of the parking space, glancing at the front door of the precinct as she drove slowly by.

Sarge stood on the steps, cell in hand.

20

Al Vincent hated working on Saturdays. He was more of the mind to play golf than hang around Optimum Security making sure everyone did their jobs. Besides, that's why he hired Vinnie Alberico—that, and because Vinnie wasn't the sharpest knife in the drawer. Truth was his stalwart employee was nothing but a thug, and a stupid one at that. The only reason he worked there was because Vincent had one over on him—one false move, and Alberico would be back in the slammer. It really was a perfect situation—unless, of course, Alberico did something stupid.

When he first brought Alberico on board, he seriously questioned whether he made the right decision. Repeating things two and three times started to get on his nerves after the first week, and Vincent was about to call it quits. But, something happened between week one and two, and Vinnie had moments of above-normal intelligence. Vincent figured he had some worth to him, so he may as well get him through the training to see how well he did.

That was several years ago.

It was fortunate Al was so patient and understanding—Alberico turned out to be a valued employee on and off the clock.

That afternoon's round was one of his best—even though it were early Spring, he hit the ball as if no time elapsed since the first snow. Buddies at the country club offered kudos whenever they could and, Al being the stand-up guy he was, accepted without giving anything in return.

The last ball in the cup at eighteen, as dusk spread the foursome headed to the clubhouse for a drink, prepared to brag or drum up pathetic excuses for their individual scores. Al brought up the rear as he checked his vibrating cell.

"Vincent."

"Get your ass over here now . . ." The voice on the other end offered no explanation.

"Now? I was just . . ."

"I don't care what you're doing—and bring Alberico with you."

"Alberico? He's working . . ."

"I don't give a shit—you have thirty minutes."

Al Vincent watched the screen of his cell fade to black. *Damn it! What did that dumb shit Alberico do now?*

21

On his own, Ryan decided to take a spin out to the house where Colbie and he suspected Alvin and Remington were keeping Brian. He wasn't sure what he might find, but it was worth a shot. Besides, Colbie had so much on her plate, it was the least he could do for her—and, Brian. He had a new respect for Colbie as she meticulously prepared her case against Alvin MacGregor and Nicole Remington. Her tenacity was inspiring and, to help, Ryan figured he could step up his game. They were now into the fourth week of Brian's disappearance and, for the first time, he felt as if they were gaining ground. Colbie did, too.

He slowed as he pulled onto the road where the crazy lady with the dog lived. *She was a freakin' nut*, he thought as he drove past her driveway. He approached from a different direction this time, offering him the opportunity to see the right side of her house instead of the left. A large dog run extended the length of the home, a large German Shepard dozing by its gate. Also visible from the road, the back yard was lush with green Spring grass—the kind that looks and feels like velvet. Further back, a dilapidated chicken coop was about fifteen feet from a patch of ground that appeared recently tilled for a garden. All in all, it wasn't a bad place, and Ryan could understand why she wouldn't want to leave. She had every right to refuse Remington's hard sell, even though Remington wouldn't take no for an answer.

As he drove by, the woman was on her knees in the front yard, weeding a flower bed under a large picture window. He sped up slightly, causing her to turn for a good look at whomever was taking a little too much time driving past her home. Ryan thought he noticed momentary recognition register on her face, but he couldn't be sure—she wasn't the most pleasant woman in the world, so it could have been her natural look for all he knew.

A quarter mile up the road was the soon-to-be overgrown dirt drive leading to the house where Remington kept Brian. Weeds were starting their march on both sides of the narrow lane, and it wasn't a stretch to imagine the drive being totally obscured in a matter of a couple of months. He drove past slowly, trying to snag a glimpse of what lay around the slight bend in the lane—he thought he saw a car, but it turned out to be a rusty, abandoned John Deere. What he really needed to do was park, and walk—perhaps a bad idea, if anyone saw him. Nonetheless, he didn't have a place to park other than the side of the road—but, with his luck, as soon as he did that, he was certain to have the only cop for fifty miles around slap him with a ticket. No, his best bet was to double back to ask the crazy woman if he could park in her driveway for about twenty minutes.

On the surface it was the worst idea Ryan ever had—obscured were the positive aspects of such an encounter. *Maybe I can get her talking*, he thought, as he weighed the pros and cons. *On the other hand, I might get shot—a definite con.* He had a hard time ignoring the shotgun, and how easily she handled it. Not to mention the dog. *That damned dog.* Colbie told him the story of how she got the large scar on her arm and, since then, he wasn't wild about dogs, at all—he was a cat man.

But, no matter how many reasons Ryan concocted for not returning to the crazy woman's house, none dissuaded him from doing what he must. He turned around at the next available spot, and headed back the other way.

****

Al Vincent and Vinnie Alberico were in hot water, each for different reasons, and they knew it. Al wasn't thrilled about being called on the carpet for Alberico, yet he had his own actions to consider. If someone found out about his bilking the business owners on the south side, it would mean the end of his cop career. The more he thought about it, however, he didn't see how that could possibly be—he made it clear to each of them if they spilled their guts about who he was, there would be hell to pay. Alvin MacGregor had them quaking in their boots every time he walked in their doors, and they counted the minutes until he left. So, that couldn't be it. Remington? Possibly, but not likely. She had too much at stake, and he was pretty sure prison wasn't on her list of things to do.

Vincent drove like hell to reach Optimum, dragged Alberico from the break room, and hightailed it to the designated meeting place. Vinnie wasn't thrilled with the idea of appearing before their boss, and he had a pretty good idea of what it was about—that bitch, Tammy. He knew he should have taken her out when he had the chance—but, she swore she wouldn't tell anyone.

And, that's where he made his mistake.

He assumed the lovely receptionist was stupid. He believed her when she said she wouldn't tell anyone and, as he slipped out the back door of her cute little bungalow, he reiterated he'd come back to kill her if she started flapping her jaws. *That should have done it*, he thought as they drove to the outskirts of the city—yet, the pit in his stomach alerted him to the possibility of his heading back to the slammer.

Soon.

****

Ryan pulled into the crazy woman's driveway, but hesitated to get out. He checked to make certain the dog was still in the outdoor run before he rolled his window down all the way to ask permission to park there for a few minutes.

"Park here? What for?" She stood, her ample frame muscled from country life.

"I just need to walk up the road a bit, and I don't want to risk getting a ticket if I park on the side." So far, she didn't seem to recognize him.

She walked toward his car, trowel in hand. "Ain't you that guy who was here about a month ago? Asking about that bitch Remington?"

Busted. "Yes—you were kind enough to give me some information then. I really appreciated it . . ." He glanced over at the side of the house—the dog was still in the pen. "Do you mind if I get out? I remember you have a pretty good-sized dog!" He flashed his toothiest grin.

The woman launched a belly laugh that would rival a man's twice her size. "I remember—you were scared shitless!" The thought of Ryan's bee lining it to his car made her shoulders shake with silent laughter.

"You know I was scared! I'm a cat guy, myself!"

"Well, I got me a couple of cats, so you can't be all that bad! Get out—I promise I'll keep him penned."

Thank God, he thought as he opened the car door. He headed immediately toward her, hand extended.

"Thank you—my name is Ryan. I'm not sure if I told you the first time I was here."

She shook his hand as if she's spent years as a lumberjack, then motioned for him to take a seat in a chair on the porch.

"I ain't got nothin' to drink 'cept water . . ."

"That's okay—thanks, anyway. I appreciate your letting me park here for a few minutes."

"What do you want up at that old house, anyway?"

He wasn't sure what to say—if he lied, he had the feeling she'd know the second the words came out of his mouth. She was a smart old bird, and it was his guess she didn't miss much.

He opted for the truth—but only as much as he was willing to dole out. "The only thing I can tell you is it has to do with Nicole Remington. I wish I could tell you more, but believe me when I say there's something going on at that house." Ryan hoped by mentioning Remington's name the woman would forget about everything else.

"Remington? What's she up to now? Trying to jack people out of their land is my guess . . ."

"Look, it's really important you don't mention I was here. If you do, we might ruin our chances to expose her."

"Expose her? For what? The bitch she is?"

"Well, that, and a few other things—are you with me? I promise I'll come back after it's all over to let you know what happened. Deal?"

The woman looked him in the eye. "Deal."

A few minutes later, Ryan pulled his car out of sight behind her house, and started to hoof it toward the house at the end of the lane. On his drive back to the crazy woman's, he scoped out the fence line to see if there were an obvious way to get closer to the hidden house without someone discovering him. Some of the fencing was barbed wire, while other parts were broken down slats in need of paint. Judging from how nicely the crazy woman kept her home, he figured the property belonged to the house down the lane.

He hugged the treeline as he made his way toward a spot in the fence with a gaping hole. A few cars passed, paying him no mind, but it was the black sedan turning into the lane in front of him that caught his attention. He stopped and crouched in an effort to blend into the thickening bushes, keeping an eye on the car for as long as he could. As the vehicle proceeded out of sight, he heard gravel crunch as it rounded the curve. From what he could see, there was only the driver who looked to be middle aged—hard to tell from his vantage point and distance. One thing was clear, though—the driver meant to go to that location. He didn't stop at the end of the drive as if he were trying to figure out his next move. He didn't take out a map—no, the driver pulled in as if he knew exactly what was down that disappearing lane.

Within moments of the black sedan's arrival, a second car pulled into the lane in the same manner. They knew where they were, and they undoubtedly were meeting the first guy—although that was total speculation. Ryan waited a few minutes before continuing toward the break in the fence—if he could get close enough to the house to see who was there, he could bust Colbie's case wide open.

Within moments he reached the hole, its gap smaller than it looked from the road, offering just enough room to climb through without scraping his back on the splintered wood and barbs. A narrow game trail paralleled the lane for a quarter of a mile, disappearing altogether as it neared the house. He thought it wise to hang back, assessing his surroundings before inching closer—from what he could see, the black sedan was parked by the side of a small shed, the second car parked just off the side of the lane. Three men stood in front of the sedan, the older guy gesturing wildly. *Holy shit*! *Is that who I think it is*? He squinted to get a better look, immediately recognizing one of the men as the cop he surveilled on the south side. *Colbie was right*! Alvin and the older man were yelling, but not loudly enough for Ryan to hear or understand the gist of what they were saying—both were pissed, and Alberico stood there like a petulant child.

Ryan scanned the area to see if he could get closer, but it was too risky. The older guy was armed with what looked like a Glock, and he was sure MacGregor completed his ensemble with a thirty-eight Smith and Wesson stashed under his golf sweater. Alberico didn't seem to be carrying—he just looked like an idiot, head down as if he were being scolded by his mother. He hadn't thought to bring a camera, so his cell phone would have to do. He snapped pictures of the men and their cars, twenty in all.

He watched for no longer than five minutes before the men got in their cars, Alvin spewing gravel and dirt as he and Alberico sped off. The older guy sat in his car for a moment as if trying to make sense of the conversation that just took place. Ryan tried to place him, but he was sure he'd never seen him before. He made a mental note of the license plate number as the man drove past him, thinking Colbie may be able to run the plate as she did when they were first investigating Remington.

He checked his watch—he told the crazy woman he would be back within twenty or thirty minutes, but he sure as hell didn't count on this happening. Still, he didn't want to break his word—she seemed the type who held a grudge, and he didn't want to be on her bad side.

Before retracing the game trail back to the fence, he snapped a few more pictures of the house and surrounding area. *Thank God for technology*, he thought, as he tucked the phone in his shirt pocket.

22

When Ryan called, Colbie was analyzing the client list as well as other documents in the two Optimum files.

"You're never going to believe where I was today . . ." Granted, it was a dramatic lead-in, but he couldn't resist.

Colbie, however, wasn't in the mood to play games. "Okay, I give—where were you?"

"At the house . . ."

At first it didn't register. "House? What house?"

"What do you mean 'what house?' The house where they're keeping Brian!"

"What? You were there?"

"Yep—I figured I didn't have anything better to do on a Saturday, so I thought I'd take a drive. Funny how I wound up out in the country . . ."

"Are you crazy? You could have gotten yourself killed!" Colbie was painfully aware of how dangerous Alvin was, and she didn't want Ryan getting himself into a difficult situation.

"Spare me—do you want to hear what happened, or not?"

"Be here in an hour . . ."

****

By the time Ryan arrived, there was a full pot of coffee brewing, and Colbie scrounged up what was left of a half dozen muffins she bought the day before. Truth be told, she wasn't happy with Ryan for taking off on his own—Alvin MacGregor couldn't be trusted, and Colbie knew all too well he was capable of anything. But, since nothing happened, she couldn't wait to hear what Ryan discovered.

Headlights reflected on the window as he pulled in, and she held the door for him with a cup of coffee in hand.

"Here—with this rain, I figured you might like something warm."

"Thanks—it's not raining hard, but it's enough to make me cold . . ." He shook the water from his jacket outside, then hung it up on a hook beside the back door. As he took the cup from Colbie, he lifted it in a toast. "Here's to taking that S.O.B. down . . ."

"Here, here . . ." She pulled out a chair at the table, and motioned for Ryan to do the same. "Okay—shoot."

Ryan made himself comfortable before recounting a detailed description of what he saw and heard, crazy woman included. Colbie listened as he described Alvin, Alberico, and the mystery man.

"Do you have any idea of who the mystery man is?"

"No, but I have a nagging suspicion I've either seen or heard of him before. From what I could hear—mind you, they were about forty feet from me—his voice sounded familiar. I thought about it on the drive home, and I just can't place him."

"Did you take your camera?"

"No . . ."

Colbie's heart sunk as she realized she'd have to rely on Ryan's memory for a complete description of the men.

"But—I had my cell . . ."

"What? You got pictures?" She shot Ryan her best 'I'll get you for that look.'

"I couldn't resist—anyway, I zoomed in as far as I could . . ." He handed Colbie his phone, the first of twenty pictures geared up on the screen.

Colbie took the phone, putting down her coffee cup as she began to scroll through the photos. Ryan noticed her fingers trembling as she put her cup on the table, staring at one of the pictures.

"What? What's wrong?" Ryan watched Colbie's face blanch as she realized the depth of their investigation.

"Excuse me . . ." She bolted from her chair, barely making it to the bathroom before violently retching. He heard the toilet flush, and he wasn't quite sure what to do—he wanted to comfort her, but it wasn't his place.

Finally she returned, her face an ashen white.

"What the hell just happened?" He was even more concerned as he looked at her.

Colbie sat, barely able to speak. "The mystery man," she whispered. "The mystery man is . . . Sarge."

23

Al Vincent was livid! He always knew Alberico was stupid, but he didn't think he was *that* stupid. He warned that dumb shit more than once to keep his hands off the female employees, and Alberico swore he wouldn't do it again. Optimum was lucky Kellie Marchand didn't file charges against the company, Alberico—or both—and Vincent ordered Vinnie to keep his nose clean.

Obviously, that was impossible.

The question was what to do about it—and, what to do about Alberico? Tammy was supposed to return to work in a couple of days—she called the day of the assault saying she had the flu, and it would be at least a few days before she would be well enough to come to work. *That was a bullshit line if I ever heard one,* he thought as he sped toward the city. The obvious solution was to make sure Alberico and Tammy didn't collide, but he couldn't count on that. If she had a mind to, Tammy could sue the company, causing it to implode. No, it seemed the wiser choice to treat Tammy like gold.

Alberico? That was a different story . . .

Vincent glanced at his passenger who sat silently, eyes glued to his cell. *Probably playing some stupid video game,* he thought, as he realized how much he detested the man sitting next to him. He had no patience for stupidity, especially when it put his operation in danger. Rifkin ordered him to make it right, no matter the method, and gave him twenty-four hours to do it. Rifkin also told him he—Alvin—was expendable, placing him in a position completely foreign to him.

As they neared the city, Al Vincent was clear about how he could make things go away—swerving onto a dirt road leading to nowhere, he was confident in his decision. Somewhere between weather beaten mile markers seven and twelve, he pulled over to the side of the road, Alberico by then asleep in the front seat. Vincent got out, and surveyed the area—to the east was an abandoned quarry, to the west a deep ravine.

Both on a seldom-traveled road.

He yanked Alberico from his seat, marched him to the ravine, and put a bullet in his brain with a gun he lifted from the evidence room at the precinct. Kicking him into the depths with his steel-toed boot, he watched Alberico's body tumble and roll to the bottom. *Good riddance,* he thought as Vinnie's body came to rest against a jagged boulder.

He strode back to his car, his mind already on putting the screws to Colbie Colleen.

24

Colbie still couldn't believe the deep breach of trust permeating the precinct. Seeing the photo of Sarge, Alvin, and Alberico was a roundhouse to her gut, and she couldn't think of a time when she felt more betrayed.

She lay in bed the following morning thinking about how she needed to proceed—considering two of the top officers in the precinct were knee-deep in corruption, she also had to consider how many other officers may be involved. There was no question she had to report it to Internal Affairs—she had the proof, and the sooner the better. First, however, she needed a face-to-face with Nicole Remington. She grabbed her glasses from the nightstand, and dialed. It was early—only seven-thirty—but she didn't care.

"Nicole? This is Colbie—I need to see you immediately."

"What? Why? What's happened?"

I'm not comfortable discussing this over the airwaves—

how about we meet at the coffee shop at First and Cross? Nine o'clock?"

"How about nine-fifteen? I need to work around a previous appointment."

To Colbie, fifteen minutes didn't make a difference one way or the other. "I'll see you there at nine-fifteen—and, Nicole? Don't mention our meeting to anyone—don't even tell anyone you have an appointment. Understand?"

Nicole detected something different in Colbie's voice—something frightening.

"I'll see you at nine-fifteen."

****

Al Vincent pulled open the door to Optimum Security early that morning thinking about the lonely road. As satisfying as it was to kick Alberico to his grave, he knew his actions could have serious ramifications—especially if someone happened upon the body. But, it was a risk he had to take—and, if luck were on his side, critters and scavengers would work their magic before anyone could recognize him. He hadn't told Rifkin yet, and chances were good he wasn't going to be pleased—but, the way Vincent saw it, Alberico was nothing but an irritating, puny piss ant with little to offer anyone—especially him. Certainly a viable reason . . .

He wasn't sure when Tammy would make it back to work, but, when she did, he had to make sure he treated her with respect. He was confident she didn't know anything, so there wasn't a reason to drag her into the whole thing—

besides, if that happened, he'd probably have to get rid of her, too. The last thing he wanted, though, was 'serial killer' plastered next to his name on a wanted poster—but if it meant saving his own ass, then he'd do whatever.

Vincent didn't bother with his own office—he first rifled through Tammy's files to see if he needed to suspect her—nothing. Her desk contained files found at any receptionist's desk and, as far as he could tell, everything was in order. He was sure Tammy was everything she appeared to be—a single mom, working her butt off to make ends meet.

Next, Alberico's office. It was a surprise that Alberico was actually doing a good job for Optimum—his files were in order, but Vincent did wonder about the client list with handwritten names on the last page. He didn't know any of them, but he suspected they may be prospective marks for Optimum—Mark Lofton, Nigel Crestmoor, and Kathy Simonson. He recognized the first two, but wasn't sure about the last, thinking it may be the woman he was supposed to meet at the coffee shop, but she was a no-show. Still, the names didn't concern him, and he couldn't see how any of them could possibly pose a threat to the operation.

By the time he finished combing through all the files, it was nearly eight o'clock. He grabbed a cup of coffee in the break room before heading out the door only to run into Tammy. *On a Sunday*? He was stunned at the extent of Alberico's brutality and, in that moment, he put to rest any false regrets lurking in his soul.

"Tammy! What the hell happened to you?" Playing dumb seemed the best approach.

"Hey, Al. I'd rather not go into it—I'm just stopping by to hand in my resignation." There was no reason to go into details, and the less they knew about her involvement in helping Colbie, the better off she'd be.

"Resignation? Why?" *Damn it! Now I'll have to find someone new . . .*

"I found a job closer to home, and I'll be able to spend more time with my son."

"Is it about the money? I think we can manage a substantial raise . . ." In his world, everyone could be bought.

"No—it's not the money. "

"If you need to take some time off, I understand. It looks as if you've been through a hell of a lot."

Tammy shook her head. "No—I don't think so . . . here's my resignation letter." She handed him a sealed envelope, thanked him for the opportunity to work at Optimum, and headed out the door.

Class act, he thought, flipping the letter on the receptionist's desk. *Can't say I blame her . . .*

****

Remington was right on time. *She looks older,* Colbie thought as she walked through door and made her way to Colbie's table.

"Okay—I'm here. What's so important?" Nicole didn't bother to take off her coat.

"Thanks for meeting me—I want to tell you in person what's going on . . . and, it's all about to come to a head."

Nicole sat up a bit straighter. "What do you mean?"

"I'll tell you on the way, but, right now, I need you to take me to Brian."

"I can't do that! Al will kill me—literally!"

"You don't understand—it's over, and I'm trying to save your skin. Remember when I told you things were going to hit the fan? Well, they have . . ."

Remington stared at Colbie as if she saw an apparition of Al Vincent standing in front of her. "But . . ."

"There are no 'buts,' Nicole—take me to him, now."

Colbie's gut told her things were going to move quickly, and she wanted to honor her promise to Remington to help her get out as unscathed as possible. Alvin MacGregor played her for a fool and a patsy and, although Nicole had her own skeletons, Colbie felt prosecutors could negotiate her involvement down to something minor in exchange for her help in the investigation. Or course, there were no guarantees, but with Colbie's throwing in a good word, she was confident Nicole would come out smelling like a rose.

Without a word, Nicole got up and started for the door. "Follow me, she directed. "I'm in the brown BMW . . ."

"I know what car you drive . . ." Colbie offered, just to make certain Remington didn't mistake who was in charge.

****

Alvin strode up the precinct steps as if nothing happened. It was nearly empty, filled with only a skeleton crew because of its being a Sunday. He arranged to meet Rifkin in his office to hash out their next move and, as far as he could tell, there was nothing else he could do but tell him about Alberico. *He's gonna be pissed,* he thought as he waited for Rifkin in his office. *But, once he realizes Alberico was a loose cannon, he'll see it was the best thing to do.*

Five minutes passed until Rifkin closed his office door behind him. He grabbed a bottled water from the fridge, sat down at his desk, and glared at Alvin.

"This better be good . . ." Rifkin waited for Alvin to bring him up to speed.

Better to get it done. "Alberico's dead."

"What do you mean—dead? What the hell happened? He sure as hell was okay yesterday . . ."

"I know. But, after we left the farmhouse, I gave serious thought to what was happening, and I couldn't shake the feeling that things are about to go south."

"Go south? Why?"

"I don't know—just a gut feeling."

"A gut feeling? That tells me nothing other than you sound like that bitch, Colbie Colleen—but, I see your point. With Alberico out of the way, what do we have to worry about? Nobody knows anything—unless you're talking about Remington . . ."

"It's no secret Alberico was a dumb shit and, with him out of the way, we may be able to fly under the radar. Still . . ." Alvin bristled at Rifkin's comment of his being like Colbie, but chose to let it go—dissension among the ranks was the last thing they needed. He was also positive

Remington didn't know crap about anything other than the oil reserves operation. She wasn't that smart, and he took every precaution to keep her in the dark.

Rifkin glared at MacGregor from across his desk. "Brian—he's gotta go."

"I have some ideas . . ." Alvin returned the glare.

****

Colbie followed Remington to the country road leading to the farmhouse. When she was there the first time, she approached from the south. That day, however, Remington took another route, past the crazy woman's house, turning right instead of left onto the lane leading to the farmhouse. *This must be the route Ryan took—he mentioned seeing the dog run on the side of the nutball's house.* As she drove past, she noticed the woman in the front yard, mowing a small patch of grass with an ancient rotary two-bladed manual mower. The whole area had a creepy feel to it, and Colbie wasn't sure what to expect as she pulled up beside Remington's car.

The outside of the farmhouse looked as if it hadn't seen a speck of paint for decades. The front porch—probably a 'veranda' at some time—sagged, corner pillars straining under the weight of a shambled roof. As Colbie climbed out of her car, she noticed a cat streaking across the what once was a manicured lawn, on its way to a barn at the back of the property.

Colbie wasted no time. "Take me to him," she ordered, as Remington led her to the back of the house. Three broken steps led to a screened back door hanging from its hinges, a foul odor assaulting their senses as Remington unlocked the door.

There he was—shackled to a chair in a windowless room at the end of the hall. Remington stepped aside as Colbie entered. "He's right there . . ."

"Oh, my God—Brian!" As a cop, she knew better than to announce her arrival, but she couldn't help herself as relief rushed through her. She knew Alvin MacGregor too well and, until she saw Brian alive, she wasn't sure what to expect.

Brian raised his head, turning slightly as he looked toward the voice at the front door. His health deteriorated severely since the previous week, and it became clear to him the head of the operation had no intention of letting him go. All he could count on was Colbie . . .

As much as Colbie wanted to rush to him, the cop in her surfaced. She had to consider Remington's proclivity for weakness—there was a chance she clued Alvin into the progress of Colbie's investigation, and she couldn't take a chance. She carefully drew her thirty-eight from its shoulder holster, gripping it in classic cop style.

"Stay here," she ordered Remington as she inched down the hallway.

Remington was all too happy to comply.

Colbie called to Brian, as she assessed her situation—two rooms to her left and one to her right serving as an ambush point was a real possibility. "Brian—it's Colbie. Can you hear me?"

Brian nodded. "Colbie!"

"Is there anyone in there with you?" Her question exposed possible risk—if anyone were in the room with him, he or she could easily blow his brains out without a second thought. Hers, too. She had no doubt Alvin and Sarge were capable of doing just that.

Brian's voice gained strength as he called out to her. "No—no one's here."

"When was the last time you saw anyone?" She figured Brian would know if someone were lurking in any of the rooms flanking the hall, setting up an ultimate choke point once she entered the room in which Brian sat cuffed to a chair.

"Yesterday . . ."

Colbie continued to move forward as if she were a member of a trained SWAT team, her cop instincts in full swing. She scouted each room in the hall and, as she reached Brian's room, she violently kicked the door open to its fullest width, strafing her weapon from left to right.

Empty.

She rushed to Brian, assessing the extent of his injuries—handcuffs shackled his wrists to the back of the chair, his feet secured with two, long zip ties. Spittle stained the front of his shirt, and he barely had the strength to look at her.

"It's over," she promised, motioning to Remington to give her the key to the handcuffs. Remington obliged, then stepped back toward the doorway as if she couldn't stand to be close to either of them. Truth was she was scared to death something would go down and, if she stood close to the door, at least she had a fighting chance to get out.

Turned out it was a good plan, but one that didn't work. Before she reached the hall, Alvin and Sarge bulled through the screen door, weapons drawn.

"Get over there!" Alvin ordered, his weapon trained on her as she retreated to a place beside Colbie and Brian. Remington's face drained as she realized he had no intention of leaving witnesses. She knew that look—an unwavering determination to have his way, no matter what.

Sarge aimed his weapon at Colbie as if he felt nothing for her. "Drop your weapon, Colbie—don't do anything stupid. You can't get out of this, so you may as well make it easy on yourself—and, lover boy there." He sounded like a perp in a grade B movie.

"How can you do this? You're a cop, for God's sake!"

"For Christ's sake—spare me the sanctimonious crap. Why do you think?"

"Money? Is that it? Is that what seduced you into giving up your career?" Colbie couldn't believe what she was hearing—she barely recognized the two men standing before her.

"It's a powerful motivator—you know that. The opportunity presented itself, and I went for it."

Alvin kept his weapon trained on Remington as Colbie turned her attention to him. "Why, Alvin? What did I ever do to you?"

"Ah . . . that's a rich one! What did you do to me? Let's see . . . every day I had to watch you climb through the ranks, leaving me to do your dirty work."

"What the hell are you talking about?"

"You know exactly what I'm talking about—with you around, I couldn't trust you wouldn't find out about my—extracurricular—activities. After you left the precinct, I still couldn't get rid of you . . . so, I decided it was time to knock you off that damned high horse of yours."

"That's when you decided to kidnap Brian? Just to get back at me?"

"Shut up, Colbie!" Sarge commanded, his voice strong and determined.

Colbie intuitively sized up her situation. There was no question Alvin was a walking time bomb, and she had no doubt he'd go off the deep end with the slightest provocation. Sarge, on the other hand, was a crapshoot. Clearly she didn't know him, at all . . .

"You know, of course, you're not going to walk out of here . . ." Colbie thought she saw a flicker of regret cross his face, but after a moment she recognized she was mistaken.

Remington started to cry as she realized her fate.

As Colbie stared down the barrel of Sarge's gun, a shadow moved behind him.

"Neither are you . . ." barked an unfamiliar voice. Two rapid fire shotgun blasts from a sawed off twelve gauge ripped into the backs of Alvin and Rifkin, blowing gaping holes into their crumpling bodies.

Colbie hit the floor, grabbing Brian's chair so he would topple with her. "Get down!" she screamed as Remington stood like a deer in the headlights.

Colbie lifted her head to get a good look at the silhouetted shadow standing in the doorway. The crazy woman with the dog!

“Get up—I ain’t gonna hurt you, she promised, lowering the shotgun to her side.

Colbie got to her knees, eyes trained on the figure at the door. Still not certain, she clutched her weapon, but intuition told her the woman was on their side. Pooling blood and innards littered the floor, mingling with the disgusting remnants of feces and stale food. Remington’s face was spattered with bits of Alvin.

“Who are you . . .” Colbie had a good idea, but she still wasn’t sure why she showed up when she did.

“I live down the road—I seen the cars pulling into the driveway, and I knew somethin’ was up. I came through the back woods, and when I heard one of these guys . . .” She motioned to the bodies splayed on the floor. “I figured someone was in trouble. There ain’t been nothing but trouble since she started sniffing around.” The crazy woman pointed the shotgun at Remington who still knelt on the floor, uncertain of her fate. That old broad hated her guts, and if she could take out two cops with a shotgun, she sure as hell could wipe her out, too.

“He made me do it . . .” she confessed.

“I figured—you ain’t smart enough to think this up on your own.” Remington wasn’t certain if she should be offended by the woman’s comment.

Colbie got up, surveying the bloodbath and bodies before her. “She’s right—she didn’t know about any of this until today—none of this is her fault.” She looked at the woman, offering a silent thank you—if she hadn’t shown up when she did, things would have turned out differently.

"Alright, then." The woman lowered the shotgun, and Colbie heard Remington's relief.

"Please stay where you are—I have to report this." Colbie turned to Brian, her face filled with apology.

"Unfortunately, that goes for you, too—I'll undo the cuffs and ties, but you have to sit there in order to preserve evidence. Can you do that? Can you hang in there until an ambulance arrives?"

Brian nodded. "I can do anything you need . . ."

Colbie took his head in her hands, placing a soft kiss on his forehead. "Not much longer, she whispered. Not much longer . . . "

25

Colbie and Brian sat at their kitchen table much as they did the day he left for his hiking trip three months previous—only, this time, they were together. As one. No more burying their heads in textbooks, or anything else to distract them from the obvious.

They were meant to be together.

Thanks to a few days in the hospital, plus Colbie's good cooking, Brian's recovery was rapid. She took time off from school to care for him and, by the time the first day of summer rolled around, he was back to his old self. Of course, there would never be a way to erase what happened, but headlines were beginning to fade. For the first time in months, he felt as if his life were back on track—especially with Colbie.

After the events at the farmhouse, accusations swirled around the police department, giving rise to a full-blown investigation. Heads rolled, and several of Colbie's previous compatriots were awaiting trial, their futures to be decided months down the road when they would once again be headline material. Yet, with those individuals gone, the precinct somehow managed to right itself, once again striving for respect from its community.

The real victim was not only Brian, but Nicole Remington, as well. Colbie surmised she would probably never be the same after her last five years under the thumb of Alvin MacGregor. As they left the farmhouse that day, it was clear Remington's life changed—forever shattered by greed. Colbie was true to her word, helping her as much as she could by attesting to Remington's willingness to help in Colbie's investigation. Immunity? Maybe, but doubtful. She knew it, and Remington knew it. Chances were good, though, her punishment would amount to little more than a slap on the wrist.

A forceful knock at the back door interrupted their conversation, as Ryan poked his head in.

"Anybody home?"

"Hey! C'mon in! Coffee?" Colbie jumped up to grab an extra cup.

"Of course—got any donuts?"

"Donuts? No—how about some toast?"

"I'll take it!" Ryan pulled up an extra chair to the small table. "So—I have news . . ."

Brian knew his friend well—for him to make a special trip to announce something, it had to be big. "What kind of news?"

"Well—I got a job offer on the East Coast, and I accepted."

Colbie froze, mid-pour.

"Nice! What's the job?" As his best friend, Brian noticed something was missing as Ryan launched into the particulars of his new position.

". . . so, all in all, I think it will be good for me!" Ryan paused, searching Colbie's face for reaction." "What do you think?"

"What do I think? Well, of course we'll miss you, but if you're excited about it, then we're excited about it!"

Brian enthusiastically agreed with her, clapping his friend on the shoulder on his way out of the room. "I'll be right back . . ."

Colbie handed Ryan his coffee, then leaned against the counter, waiting for the toast to pop up.

"Really, Ryan? The East Coast? Why?"

"I have my reasons . . ."

She peered at him from over her cup, searching his face for an answer.

"Hey, you know—can I take a rain check on the toast? I just remembered something I have to do . . ." Ryan grabbed his jacket from the hook by the door, lingering so close he could smell the slight fragrance of perfume.

She couldn't look at him. "When do you leave?"

Ryan cupped her face in his hands. "Tomorrow," he whispered. "I leave tomorrow . . ."

Then, he was gone.

Faith Wood

CPS, Behaviorist

Faith Wood is a Behaviorist, Certified Professional Speaker, Hypnotist, and Handwriting Analyst. Her interest in Behavior Psychology blossomed during her law enforcement career when it occurred to her if she knew what people really wanted, as well as motives behind their actions, she would be more effective in work and life. So, she hung up her cuffs, trading them in for traveling the world speaking to audiences to help them better understand human behaviors, and how they impact others. Wood speaks about how to tap into the area of the brain that controls actions which, in turn, have a tendency to adjust perceptions, thereby launching a more empowered life.

Faith Wood touches lives, and leaves a lasting impression. A mother of four, she lives with her husband in Airdrie, Alberta, Canada.

Visit Faith's website, www.faithwood.com, to learn more about her, and her services. She helps people worldwide change their lives, and she can help you.

Unleash the power of Faith!

CHRYSALIS PUBLISHING AUTHOR SERVICES
EDITOR: L.A. O'NEIL
chrysalispub@gmail.com

COVER ART
JEN KRAMP STUDIOS
jenkramp@gmail.com

Made in the USA
Columbia, SC
07 October 2017